# FESTIVAL OF VENUS

## Anonymous

CW00607132

Nexus

First published in Great Britain in 1992 by
Nexus
338 Ladbroke Grove
London W10 5AH

First published in the United States of America by
Masquerade Books, Inc.

Copyright © Masquerade Books, Inc. 1991

ISBN 0 352 32801 0

A catalogue record for this title is available from the
British Library

Printed and bound in Great Britain by
Cox & Wyman Ltd, Reading, Berks.

# FESTIVAL OF VENUS

# PROLOGUE

Brigeen Mooney stood barefoot in the bright sunlight of a summer's soft evening, turning the last of the cattle from the hill as the Angelus bell began its sonorous tolling. She deliberated irresolutely within herself whether or not to make the sign of the cross, then lifted her hand to her breasts hesitantly before stamping her slim foot into the poached mire and spitting in the direction of Moygara chapel, the source of the bell.

A minute before she had been lighthearted and carefree, the future far from her mind. Now she stood trembling with anger and outrage, heedless of the heartbreaking beauty of Lough Bara, illuminated by the long golden rays of the declining sun to the east; heedless of the intricate pattern of small farms, woods, narrow lanes and ring-forts that made up her parish, spread enchantingly at her feet.

The knowledge, summoned by the bell's steady pealing in the still air, that she was destined, against her own desires, to become a nun, appalled and terrified her. Biting her lip, Brigeen's vivid imagination pictured a world without sunlight, without laughter, without the hope of escape except by death.

She sat a moment on a stone and a sinister thought occurred to her. She would run away! Yes, that was the only solution.

She thought of the few nuns whom she had met—dry and crabbish spinsters, lifelong brides of Christ. She laughed bitterly. And the laughter grew more and more riotous as she began to scheme her escape. She thought suddenly of the dowry her father would be called on to pay to consign her to the con-

5

vent. Her father had showed her the bag of money (worth the better part of the herd) only the night before. She would steal it tonight. There was certainly enough to get her far away from the clutches of her family. It would be delicious revenge on the two women who had, in cold, self-righteous piety conspired to immure her, Brigeen Mooney, behind the cold stone walls of a convent. At once she pictured her mother and her great-aunt gossiping together, and delighted in the violent rage the two hags would fall into upon realizing that she had escaped them.

"Damn them both, the bitches. Damn them for what they tried to do to me. The cunts! They'll be sorry." Brigeen glanced around furtively to reassure herself that no one was within earshot. There was no sign of a living soul. Even the tolling of the bell had ceased and, relieved that she had not given her state of mind away to a passerby, she rose and began a slow walk home.

All along the way she planned her escape and occasionally laughed out loud at the simplicity of it. Smiling grimly, Brigeen let her mind wander, picturing herself far from County Sligo and its poverty. In her imagining she was free from the farm, free from the wretchedness, the piety and the murmured resentments of a peasant race.

In her mind's eye, she stood proudly on the prow of a gilded Venetian barge being adroitly poled between serried ranks of palazzos and ducal mansions, the object of the multitude's acclaim and heartfelt adulation. Petals cascaded about her as she bestowed indulgent acknowledgement of her admirers' delight. She bowed from the balcony of a rococo private theatre, clad in sequins and spangles, bestowing her favor upon a small but glittering audience of handsome grand dukes, Spanish lords, and English barons.

6

"A courtesan of the highest class, a celebrated demi-goddess of the passions," she pronounced aloud, confident that her words were unheard by any save herself. As she followed the cattle along the rough lane leading to the pen, she pictured herself reclining in a curtained boudoir, scented and bejewelled, while admirers knelt to lavish kisses on her toes. She held court, swathed in thick, dark furs, in a prettily brocaded kiosk on the golden shores of the Bosphorous. An emperor's destiny rested on her merest caprice; her whim was sufficient to raise the meanest peasant to exalted rank, or have the highest in the land beheaded to the accompaniment of adoring cheers. She smiled as the executioner's scimitar rose and fell.

A shout brought her to her senses in an instant. The Grand Canal, the gilded barges and the tall kiosks faded before her eyes as her mother's voice rang harsh in her ear.

"And is it yerself at last, me girl? And all of us waiting on thee, eh? 'Tis a good thing ye are off to lead a life of ease and plenty with the nuns, Brigeen, I tell ye. Begod, ye were enough time about the beasts while yer poor mother saw to the fire and the tea. 'Twas mooning and dithering ye were, I'll be bound."

Life of ease certainly, but not with those poor wretches of Christ, thought Brigeen. And without so much as a shrug, she haughtily brushed past her mother, affecting not to hear so much as a word. She busied herself with pulling the rude gate of the small pen behind her, then knelt unceremoniously on the rough stones beside the stream which served the household for washing water.

Her hands and face washed in the cold, clear water, Brigeen pushed open the door and, stooping, entered the malodorous dark cottage that was her home.

Scarcely glancing at her parents, her great-aunt, or her numerous siblings, she bowed her head while her father, his speech slurred and hesitant, recited what he could remember of the prayer before meals.

"Good," Brigeen muttered to herself. "The old codger is drunk again. After an afternoon of tasting the poteen with his friends, he'll sleep like a dead man tonight. All the easier to take that bag of gold coins from the chest by his bed. Thank the good lord Mother sleeps like an old cow, grumbling and snoring; nothing could wake her." Brigeen was certain that success was easily within reach.

The repast, a chipped enamel bowl filled to overflowing with boiled potatoes, was consumed with indecorous haste and the unfeigned good appetites of those who spend most of their waking hours in the open air.

"Ye are to leave us next week, so?" observed Brigeen's great-aunt presently. Brigeen pointedly ignored the woman, well aware that her present troubles were due most of all to her, even more than to her mother. The elderly woman's reasoning was clear and straightforward enough, Brigeen reasoned grimly. By ensuring that her nephew's daughter took the veil, the elderly woman would attain grace in the sight of God, the Blessed Virgin, and Our Saviour himself.

Brigeen shuddered with delight. She was thwarting the greedy old woman's plan. When, in due course, her great-aunt reached the end of her earthly journey, a warm and enthusiastic welcome to God's heavenly kingdom would be denied her. Brigeen didn't feel too bad considering that when the old witch died, her parents would inherit much more than the sum of money that was necessary to admit her to the nunnery.

Later that night, Brigeen lay awake in her narrow bed at the end of the house, listening to the rhythmic, unsteady rasp of her father's breathing and her mother's frequent bouts of laboured coughing, the result of many long years of tending open turf fires.

"I am going to leave all of this behind," she murmured softly. She was excited and terrified at the same time. "I am going to live the life of a lady, not that of a wretched bride of Christ." The words made her more certain than ever that she must leave that very night.

Later, she stole apprehensively through the cottage. Brothers and sisters sighed and groaned in their sleep. She did not need to dress. She had worn her warmest clothing to bed. She tip-toed in stockinged feet toward the chest at the foot of her parents' bed. Her heart pounded in her chest. There she stood at the foot of the bed glancing first at the two figures huddled under the covers. Seeing that they slept soundly, she silently lifted the heavy oak lid of the chest. And there it was, the sack of cash for the nunnery. She did not hesitate now, and silently grabbed the cloth bag and stole out of the house before a hint of early morning light brightened the windows of the dark little cottage.

Once out in the bracing night air, Brigeen began to run. She ran as fast as she could, her long hair flying madly about her. She knew where to go, and once far enough away from any of the villagers' houses, she let out a whoop of glee. She was free! And rich! There was more money in the bag than she had ever seen in her young life. She was going to Dublin and see what fortune had in store for her. She ran exhilarated and free all night long.

9

# -1-

Brigeen laid her small suitcase on the rough blanket of the iron trestle bed and looked around her. Hers was the second bed in the room, she noted with some surprise.

She had arrived in the teeming city of Dublin that afternoon. She had traveled all night and most of the day to arrive. She had never been in such a big city, but the bustle, the crowd, had not frightened her. Rather she felt more alive than she ever had.

She had just sat down in a small pub for a warm cup of tea when a strange older woman sat down next to her. Brigeen noticed that she was older, but dressed in the finest dress she had ever seen. She was a little frightened by the lady, mostly because of her strange intensity.

"Don't be frightened, my little pet," the lady had said, smoothing her cheek. And with that little bit of comfort, Brigeen found herself crying and telling this woman her story. The older woman's lips curled up at the corners as Brigeen sobbed.

"Shhh, me little one. I'm Ursula Flannery. I have a house not too far from here where you can stay. Come, come. Stop your crying. I have many girls staying there with me to keep me...ah 'company' in my growing age."

Brigeen looked at her though teary eyes. She couldn't believe her luck.

Although she was still a bit frightened of Ursula, she decided she had nowhere else to turn. And the lady had been so nice. Ursula had paid for her tea, then ushered the poor lost girl to her "home".

Apparently she was meant to be sharing the room. She sat down on the bed. Glancing at the door to reassure herself that she was alone, she curiously examined the visible possessions of her absent companion. A pair of silver-backed hairbrushes flanked a faded daguerreotype in an oval silver frame. Brigeen whistled softly to herself; so the girl with whom she was to share came from a moneyed family, did she? Inexplicably vexed, Brigeen bit her lip; she resolved not to reveal any detail of her family's existence to the total stranger. After a moment's reflection, her glum mood was dispelled as suddenly as it had arrived; perhaps the girl with whom she had to share her room knew something of the city and would show her around. Perhaps they might even become friends. Brigeen knew no one in this strange city and that would be a great comfort to her.

She got up to study the daguerreotype. Upon closer examination she became puzzled by the image. It was of a young man wearing what appeared to be flowing robes. He held a sharp staff in one hand and a chalice in the other. He was naked and exposed his stiff member; it jutted out from the front of the robes. There was a clattering on the stairs and Brigeen jumped back to her place on the bed. She felt guilty and tried to hide it.

The door burst open. A slim girl with a boyish figure stood in the doorway, her hands on her hips and a roguish smile on her face.

"The name is Bernadette, my dear. You must be Brigeen Mooney."

The way the girl had uttered the words made it neither a statement nor a question; Brigeen contented herself with a mute nod of assent. The girl's manner puzzled her; she had expected a younger, less vivacious companion for some reason. Bernadette, her arms folded, minced delicately around Brigeen and surveyed her curiously.

"Goodness me," she exclaimed, "you are a pretty one, aren't you?"

Brigeen drew in her breath sharply as the younger girl extended a cool, slim hand and gently squeezed her breast.

"Quite a pocket Venus, my adorable girl. I count myself lucky that we ended together in this room. If you taste as good as you look, you and I shall enjoy some rare treats together."

Brigeen gasped again and said, "Whatever do you mean? I confess I am unable to grasp the sense of anything you have said so far."

Bernadette chuckled throatily and flung herself onto her bed before turning to face Brigeen with a look of mingled amusement and ill-concealed contempt writ plain on her elfish face.

"Come, Brigeen dear," she whispered, her voice soft, yet as clear as the sibilant hiss of an asp. "We are on the Emerald Isle, to be sure, but one has to draw the line somewhere; surely you are not so very green that you are ignorant about what pretty young women like us really do?"

Brigeen suddenly felt quite faint. Following Bernadette's example, she tottered over to the empty bed and sat down heavily, staring at the scornful yet pitying expression on the younger girl's face.

"No," she said at length, "No, Bernadette, I really have no idea at all. I swear by all that's Holy that whatever it is you take for granted I know is a closed book to me."

Bernadette whistled slowly and leaned over to wrench open a drawer halfway up the tall oak chest beside her bed.

"Want a cigarette, you poor, ignorant virgin? You certainly look as if one would do you good. Or would you prefer a sip of rum? Look, I still have a little left." She extracted a neat silver hip flask and tossed it nonchalantly onto Brigeen's bed. Dumbfounded and half-believing that all this was some preposterous dream, Brigeen slowly took the flask into her hands and unscrewed the top. She sniffed it cautiously, much to Bernadette's unfeigned merriment.

"Go on, goose, take a swig. I don't mind if you take a good draught of it, I can get more easily enough, you know. Still, I expect a rural primitive like yourself is more accustomed to poteen?" The inquiry was sympathetic enough in tone, but went unanswered.

Brigeen hesitantly raised the flask to her lips and let a few drops of the fiery dark liquid trickle over her tongue.

"Welcome to the dark secrets of the Old Ways," crowed Bernadette. "Go on, drink some of it, don't just play with it. Take a mouthful," Bernadette urged. By now Brigeen was beginning to feel somewhat vexed by the chiding of a girl conspicuously younger that herself, so she recklessly tilted her head and swallowed a mouthful without mishap.

"Now tell me," Brigeen said, wiping her mouth with her hand. "Whatever do you mean by 'Old Ways'?" She was quite innocent in asking, and did not expect the roar of laughter from the girl.

"Oh-ho!" exclaimed Bernadette. "I did get a fresh one." And then taking a draught from the flask, she puffed on her cigarette and regarded Brigeen mischievously. "I guess that I'll just have to educate you meself then," and laughed like a raving leprechaun. After some time Bernadette ceased her giggles and sat up to stare at Brigeen's exquisite face in the waning afternoon sunlight. Rooks cawed in the tall elms that lined the street outside the window.

"You, my dear, will probably be more sensible and tractable than I was. It seems that you are destined for more exalted things than came my way." She sighed and once more her elfin face took on a look of sadness. Brigeen longed to comfort her.

After a moment's hesitation, she joined Bernadette on the slim girl's narrow bed and put an arm around her.

"There, there," she said. "What is the matter?" To her surprise, Bernadette wriggled in her grasp as slippery as a fish and seized Brigeen in a surprisingly strong grip.

"Now that you are here, you Venus of the bogs and boreens, nothing is—or can be—the matter. Kiss me! Kiss me, Brigeen!" To Brigeen's surprise, their lips met wetly and passionately. A sharp and determined tongue invaded Brigeen's mouth. Her head reeled with the unexpected pleasure of the sensation until she wrenched herself from the younger girl's grasp and fled, her senses whirling to the window.

Sligo Bay seemed closer than Brigeen had ever seen it before—its broad sand-banks and arrow-straight dredged channel, the villages and hamlets on

16

the farther shore, the narrow spit of Oyster Island, the broad, flat expanse of Cony Island and, in the distance, the vast Atlantic sprawled beyond the Black Rock lighthouse. All these were set out before Brigeen's large brown eyes, yet she took in nothing, so confused were her feelings.

Bernadette stood beside her, her slim frame nestled close against Brigeen's womanly curves. Out of the corner of her eye, Brigeen watched a single tear course down the smooth cheek. She turned to stare at Bernadette in bemusement, quite at a loss to comprehend the reason for the younger girl's sorrowful mood.

"You're like the others, aren't you?" Bernadette sobbed. "You disdain my kisses because I hardly have a woman's body at all. Go on, say it. Say I look more like a boy if you want to. Go ahead, don't spare my feelings whatever you do." The sobbing grew louder and Brigeen had to strain to catch what Bernadette was saying now.

"You can go down to Ursula and tell her to move me out of here if that's what you want, Brigeen. Oh, she'll understand readily enough, believe me. Just tell her you want someone else to introduce you to what goes on here and show you how to take your bath and everything."

Brigeen reached out and hugged the sobbing girl to her full breasts. Yes, it was true enough. Bernadette did feel more like a boy in her arms. Yet her emotions were those of a mawkish girl, for all her mystifying utterances and her air of pretended sophistication. In one long realization, Brigeen made some sense of what the girl had said. But somehow, this was even more confusing. For the moment, though, her hands stroked the soft chestnut hair, her lips sought the trembling lips, and they embraced wetly and awkwardly, trembling with the awe of discovery of one another.

As if in a dream, Brigeen found that she was being led to her own narrow bed and pressed gently onto it; slim fingers unbuttoned her plain bodice and her cotton blouse. Moist lips softly kissed the white hillocks of her breasts and, as she drew in her breath sharply, careful teeth encircled her right nipple and gentle fingertips stroked her left. She felt as though all the strength had been drained from her; it was as if she were powerless to resist the slim forearm, bare now to the elbow, that was wriggling between her thighs and caressing her in a way that excited her beyond her powers to describe.

Nimble fingers loosened the laces of her drawers. A busy hand sped unhindered across her taut abdomen, pausing for a moment in the copse of dark curls at the junction of her smooth thighs. Before she could venture to protest, a wicked finger had unerringly found her most treasured, shameful secret and was tickling her crimson button of solitary pleasure with unerring expertise. Oh, the shame, and the pleasure of it!

Bernadette wriggled in her arms, giggling. Their lips met moistly once again and this time Brigeen could feel Bernadette's long thin fingers searching the wet folds of her secret place. Bernadette pushed her lithe body closer to the more inexperienced girl's heaving breast. Their tongues continued to search one another's mouths passionately, as Bernadette made tiny circles around Brigeen's erect and glistening clitoris. Bernadette toyed with the curls covering Brigeen's swelling Mount of Venus. She drew back a little, stopping her eager caresses to look at her new companion. Brigeen moaned and pushed her hips in an unselfconcious thrust back towards Bernadette's magical touch. Brigeen was making little animal groans. And Bernadette's fingers found their way back to Brigeen's hot pussy that was now fairly quivering with anticipation. Brigeen was rotating her fleshy hips in quick, small movements around the younger girl's fingers. She was so filled with pleasure that she was no longer aware of her new surroundings. Her entire being was concentrated on the hot little pearl between her legs that Bernadette was now massaging more quickly. They continued to kiss, pressing their young bodies close together. Bernadette moved hers in motion to match the girl who she was pleasuring so. Brigeen fought for breath as her excitement mounted. Her back arched; she moaned softly once, twice, thrice, and then a scream burst from her throat, mercifully muffled by Bernadette's clinging kisses as the world exploded around her.

Sobbing and gasping, she lay as limp as a rag doll while her eyes watched with amazement as Bernadette daintily sucked—yes, actually sucked—the fingers of the hand which had just given her so much wicked pleasure. Her head was spinning as the pert, grinning mouth darted close to her ear.

"Your cunny tastes like the ambrosia of the Olympian gods, I swear it. Oh, Brigeen, goddess of the boreens, what a treasure you are!"

Still dazed, Brigeen lay motionless as the younger girl's tireless fingers solicitously buttoned her blouse and bodice before carefully fastening her drawers.

"And now a thorough bath is called for, I think," declared Bernadette briskly, leaping to her feet as though what had just transpired was a perfectly routine occurrence in her young life.

She let herself be pulled to her feet and readily followed Bernadette down the narrow staircase to

19

the landing below. They entered a small room containing a large tub. Bernadette walked over to the object and turned some knobs at one end.

To Brigeen's surprise, scalding water cascaded unceasingly from one tap while its neighbour tried to match it with a torrent of glacial chill. It was the first time Brigeen had seen a bath, let alone taken one.

"There, you see. I have enough influence around here to procure a scalding bath for Miss Brigeen Mooney. You will not be averse to having me bathe with you, I hope?" While Bernadette chattered she busied herself with undressing Brigeen. When that task was completed, she stood back to survey the newcomer every bit as boldly as she had gazed at her so soon after her arrival.

"My dear, you possess a waist like an hourglass, a bottom so smooth and delicious that it would have delighted Caravaggio, and darling nipples that are as delicately pretty as any Leitrim wild rose. Oh, you are a picture, to be sure!"

Brigeen, delighted to find herself the object of such immoderated and poetic flattery, stood rooted to the spot as the girl before her sank to her knees on the smooth tiled floor.

Bernadette's sharp little nose brushed against the glossy curls her own fingers had so often teased in her bed at home. The girl's hands calmly pried her thighs apart and suddenly—so suddenly that she could hardly believe it was actually happening—the darting tongue was busy between the folds of her pussy.

"Bernadette! What are you doing?" The question was superfluous, as both girls well knew. There could be no question about what Bernadette's tongue was doing, or about the prize it sought. A low moan of pure animal pleasure escaped Brigeen the instant the tip of Bernadette's tongue touched the hooded clitoris Brigeen had thought she alone in the wide world possessed. Did Bernadette's expertise mean other girls had them, too?

A discreet tap at the door startled Brigeen almost out of her wits, as she later remembered. Bernadette's pert face looked up at hers in amusement. Evidently the girl had been expecting such an interruption because there was no look of dismay on her countenance.

"Our refreshments are here, I think, dear girl. Oh, you look so startled and affrighted, like a timid doe in a forest glade.".

Laughing, Bernadette sprang to her feet and opened the door sufficiently to admit a freckled hand bearing a basket from which the necks of several bottles jutted. There was a whispered exchange and the door closed once more.

"Well, goose, get in the bath. Make yourself comfortable and feast your eyes on this wood nymph revealing her charms. You have never seen another grown girl undressed, I think?"

Brigeen shook her head. She had seen her sisters of course. What was more, she had seen her younger brothers undressed many times, even if they'd been little more than babies.

Unthinkingly, she slid into the deliciously warm bath, thrilling to the new sensation, never taking her eyes off Bernadette. Pleased at the effect she was having on Brigeen, Bernadette pirouetted, her arms akimbo, before busying herself with the padded buttons that held her satin red dress in place. Easily and gracefully, she slid out of her dress, out of her silken shift and, with a wry grimace, tore off the corset which held hardly anything.

"No more than beestings, really. Still, they give me as much pleasure as your lovely white bosoms, and that's what counts, after all."

So saying, Bernadette deftly untied the strings securing her knee-length drawers and slowly lowered them, her eyes coolly fixed on those of the older girl.

"Goodness me, Bernadette, the hair on your...your...body is in the shape of a heart!"

Bernadette laughed aloud, delighted by the note of incredulity in Brigeen's voice.

"Do you like it, my dear? It was Ursula's idea. At first, she wanted me shaved altogether, but I wept so bitterly that she relented and suggested this instead."

"Bernadette!" gasped Brigeen, suddenly all but invisible below the rim of the high bath. "You mean kindly Ursula who brought me to this house? Whatever did she want to do that for?"

Bernadette laughed. "'Kindly' Ursula? You don't know what you say, my darling country wench. 'Kindly' Ursula is one of the most powerful witches in Europe. She's educated in the 'dark ways' and we all love her and are terrified of her at the same time. She takes good care of us, so long as we do what she bids. She likes little girls, she does. She once said, in my hearing, that the moist cunt of a hairless young girl tastes twice as delicious as the furry pussy of any strapping country bitch."

Brigeen gave a great start and made an immediate attempt to leave, splashing water all around.

"Now, now, calm yourself, you silly girl. You are in very good hands. Better to have wound up in our care, than wandering alone on the streets of Dublin. That's it. Look Brigeen," she said softly, attempting to distract the frightened girl.

22

Brigeen stared, wide eyed, as Bernadette's slender fingers eased asunder the salmon-pink folds of her labia. Below the chestnut curls there was a flash of gold.

"By all the saints, what on earth is that attached to you?"

"My ring. It's Ursula's proof that we belong to her. It goes right through this flap of soft flesh, you see." Brigeen stared at it, aghast.

"Christ almighty, it must have hurt dreadfully, Bernadette!" To her amazement, Bernadette laughed and shrugged her shoulders indifferently.

"A little, no more than that. You're given something to deaden the pain. After a while, you forget it is there, just as a sailor forgets the tattoos on his chest and back."

Bernadette shivered and let herself slip easily into the bath. Even in the summer months, Ireland was frequently too chilly to allow even the hardiest soul to stand naked in an unheated room for long.

"Silly me, I forgot the stout," laughed the younger girl, by now immersed to her neck in the soothing warmth of the water. Abruptly, she squirmed to a kneeling position and leaned over to take something unseen from a basket on the cold tiled floor.

Brigeen found herself staring at a pair of sleek bare buttocks.

"My God, your bottom is much skinnier than mine!"

Once again, Bernadette chuckled throatily. "As deliciously slender as any artist's male model offering himself for hire on the Spanish Steps in Rome itself, I must say that, even if I lack the pretty staff and cullions." She turned, a bottle of liquor in each hand, and beheld the expression of uncomprehending stupefaction on Brigeen's face.

"Cullions are balls, my dear. I first heard the word when someone told me the story of Noah lying drunk

23

and exposed. A pretty word and a pretty story, too. Not quite as exciting as the tale of Lot and his daughters, of course, but pretty enough all the same."

Giggling, Bernadette settled back in the bath until the water barely covered her diminutive breasts, and opened the bottles of Irish stout carefully with a heavy brass opener.

"What a pity I lack sufficient strength in my pussy muscles to open them rather more ingeniously, like the girls from other houses."

She passed a bottle to Brigeen and proceeded to drink her own noisily, almost inverting the bottle as her head tipped back. Amused, she watched Brigeen attempt to drink hers in what she guessed the girl supposed was a more decorous and ladylike manner. Furtively, her submerged foot crept forward until Brigeen coughed and spluttered with surprise as a serried rank of pink toes tweaked the curls where her thighs met.

"Open up that pretty oyster of yours and let my piglets tease you," murmured Bernadette. Too bemused to protest, Brigeen parted her thighs and shuddered as a questing big toe brushed lightly against her clitoris.

"You like that, I rather think?" Laughed her companion. "The water makes it all the nicer, too. What a joy it must be to be clean, properly clean, at last. The squalor of the Irish peasantry and sweet, sensual pleasure are inappropriate companions, as Ursula so often tells us." Bernadette paused for Brigeen to reply but no reply came.

"Of course," she continued loftily, "the earthy smell and faintly kipperish taste one relishes when lapping the cunny of a schoolgirl from the country does have its distinctive charm, once in a while." With a sudden unexpected heave, Bernadette raised

24

her haunches and did something Brigeen would not have believed possible, spattering her with water from the delicate little flower beneath her legs.

"How on earth did you do that?" she cried aloud, impressed.

Bernadette shrieked with merriment. "Ever so easily, my darling. Flex your inner muscles a few times and you can feel the water gradually flooding in. When you want to expel it, squeeze hard enough and it shoots out, just like pressing the handle of a soda syphon. Rather amusing do you not think?"

Brigeen's confused musings were interrupted by an impatient knock on the bathroom door.

"That will be Philomena," announced Bernadette, quite unconcerned. She arose, dripping, and paced, a gleaming water sprite, to the door and admitted an olive-featured young girl. She had beautiful dark eyes and an erect carriage. She was attired in finery like Brigeen had never seen before. Her waist was drawn in tightly by a lovely corset that made her breasts seem more full. She was only wearing her underthings, but they were so fancy that Brigeen gasped in admiration.

To Brigeen's astonishment, the two young women, the one naked and dripping, the other in appealing undergarments, kissed lasciviously. Brigeen's big brown eyes widened as she saw the dark girl's hand steal between Bernadette's gleaming thighs and linger there lovingly. Bernadette wheeled abruptly and indicated Brigeen with a sweep of her thin arm.

"This is the new girl. Tell me, Philomena, is she not utterly delectable?"

The other girl fastened the brass bolt on the door and seated herself on the rim of the bath before condescending to take any notice of Brigeen, who felt highly conspicuous as she lay naked in the tub.

"Like Alice in the pool of tears," observed the newcomer in what Brigeen recognized immediately as a County Mayo accent. "Yes, Bernadette, she is quite a charmer. A virgin, I suppose?"

"But of course. I checked her carefully earlier. Still, I think she is still rather wet behind the ears, you know. She has pretty bubbies, responsive nipples, and a clitty that would melt in your mouth."

They were discussing her as if she were not there, Brigeen thought, mildly hurt. Philomena and Bernadette exchanged warm glances before the younger girl, shivering with the cold, slid into the warm water once more.

Philomena opened a bottle of stout and drained it with surprising rapidity before speaking.

"She has a lot to learn before she is sent to the Isle, mind you. Not just all the rituals and observances of our house and how to preen and display herself and such, but how to handle and suck, not to mention how to take the godemiche and petit-bonhomme without wincing. A peasant girl, is she?" Bernadette nodded in assent and Philomena grunted disdainfully.

"That ridiculous attempt at a 1910 hairstyle will have to go, of course. Rather a pity, though, since it has a certain grotesque charm on that well-shaped head. Yes, sweet Brigeen, you are a prize."

Brigeen was not a little frightened by the strange sounding words they were using. She felt that she should not ask and the mystery made her shiver a bit within. Philomena leaned toward her; she felt a dove-soft touch on her ripening breasts and trembled as the girl's thumb and forefinger squeezed her nipple savagely.

"Good. You did not squeal aloud; a promising sign, Brigeen. Tell me, do you think you can bear pain and humiliation cheerfully?" The pressure increased.

"I can try," gasped Brigeen through gritted teeth. The pain was agonizing and she could feel tears starting to come in the corners of her eyes. To her immense relief, the girl took her hand away and patted her cheek shortly.

"Women can bear quite an astonishing amount of pain. Ursula taught us that. Isn't it so, Bernadette?" The impish girl nodded. "Did Bernadette show you her little cunny ring?"

"Yes, miss," replied Brigeen, her nipple tingling. To her surprise, the sensation was pleasing.

"Good. Stand up, turn around and bend right over." The words were spoken softly, but in tones that suggested refusal would be distinctly unwise. Blushing furiously, Brigeen obeyed.

"Bend right over, girl. Open your legs full. Wider than that, child. Fully, I said." Philomena's strong hands forced Brigeen's buttocks asunder. There was a whispered conversation between Bernadette and the older woman and then a rustle as though the dark girl were searching for something amongst the lace and ruffles of her frilly underwear.

A second pair of hands, which Brigeen guessed were Bernadette's, pried the full cheeks of Brigeen's bottom even further apart. Frightened, Brigeen attempted to turn herself. As her head spun around, she glimpsed a small tapered feather in Philomena's hand. Brigeen wailed aloud as the girl's free hand slapped her rump sharply.

"Do as I say, miss. Obedience is not an affectation here, it is a command. Bend over!"

Biting her lip, Brigeen surrendered to the inevitable. A sob escaped her as the tip of the

27

feather moved softly around the puckered pink orifice of her anus and then, in response to a subtle twist to its stem, disappeared within. Bernadette chuckled throatily as she watched.

"Oh, it tickles; it burns. Take it out. Please, please take it out," moaned Brigeen, writhing.

Philomena sniggered contemptuously. "That will do for now. An inauspicious beginning, but nothing of consequence is easily begun. Continue with your bath, the pair of you. I shall see you both in my room after tea. Bernadette, do not get drunk again. A conspicuously drunken devotee is an embarrassment to all of us."

Again Brigeen was confused by the conversation between the two girls. She did not know what Philomena had meant by "devotee," and she was sufficiently bewildered and not a little excited by the strange words of these two bewitching creatures.

# -2-

Ursula raised herself on one bare elbow and looked across the broad bed at her companion, smiling sweetly.

"So the new girl shows promise, does she, Philomena? How pleasing that is. You know, the first moment I caught a glimpse of her as I walked down the street I felt quite a frisson of excitement. A perfect little Venus, you said?"

Philomena lit a delicately scented cigarette and passed it to Ursula before lighting her own, neatly inserting the tip into the ornate incense burner beside the canopied double bed.

"Very much so. She needs to be broken in, naturally, but I suspect she will need rather less vigorous birching than Bernadette required when she came to us."

"Rather a pity, really," responded Ursula. "I greatly enjoyed watching you and young Loretta belaboring that saucy minx's hindquarters until she looked like so much raw beef. Do you remember how she

30

whined and squealed when we showed her the Little Man and explained its use?"

Philomena laughed and nestled closer to the older woman, bending her head to kiss the greying long hair.

"Indeed I do, Ursula. Indeed I do. Yet she was wearing the Mystic Tree in her bottom quite contentedly a few days later with a very proud smile on her pretty little face. Once Loretta had violated her narrowest portal of love a few times with the Little Man, she was cheerful enough when that unspeakable object was shown to her."

"That ebony phallus from the temple on the Isle, you mean," laughed Ursula, letting her hand caress Philomena's long back. Philomena made a groaning noise and playfully resisted.

"Enough of that, there simply isn't time, Ursula."

Ursula persisted, not heeding the young woman's weak protest. Her hands traversed down the small of Philomena's back and rested on the rise of her pretty plump bottom. She began to tease the flesh there. Her fingers inched closer and closer to the starfished-shaped aperture that nestled there.

"No," cooed Philomena languorously. "Take your hand away this instant. If you excite me again I shall need to be licked again and we both know where that leads, do we not?"

"To me wanting a lick and maybe another light spanking, Philomena," sighed Ursula, her fingers still persisting around the puckered little anus of Philomena's lovely little arse.

Philomena raised her hips despite her earlier protests. She could not resist a little hip rotation to the gentle probing of the older woman's experienced hand.

"That's it, my pretty dove. I know you want anoth-

31

er little lick on that delicious little pearl between your legs." As Ursula was hoarsely whispering in Philomena's ear, her hand had reached up from behind and was tickling that tender spot.

"If you don't stop that, Ursula, I am going to have to give your precious bum a stiff whack. And a few lashes with my tongue, if you are really naughty."

"Oh, that's it my girl. Threaten me, but only if you promise to do as you say." And with that Ursula plunged one finger into the the rosy little anus of Philomena, while another finger sought the other opening of softer, wetter pink flesh that was protected by dark hair. Philomena yelped with glee, and reached over and began to tease Ursula's naked breasts. Although Ursula was older than the other girls, she still had an extremely youthful body. Her breasts had retained the shape and firmness of a girl barely into her twenties.

Philomena was jerking her hips over the busy hand of Ursula.

"You are being very, very bad Ursula. Oh, yes. That's it! Oh!"

Philomena, racked with powerful spasms caused by the delicious probing fingers of Ursula, threw back her head and was panting with animal pleasure. When at last her juices flowed freely, her body contracting with wonderful pulses, Ursula playfully slapped her dripping pussy. With that Philomena promptly jumped up and grabbed a brush that lay on the dressing table.

"You nasty thing. Come here." She brandished the large silver brush, and the two of them began to playfully tumble on the bed together. At last Philomena had the older woman pinned over her knee. One hand held the brush, the other held. Ursula's wrists. And then Philomena's hand wandered down the taut

32

backside that was exposed to her. She patted them lightly at first, and Ursula cooed a bit.

"You like that, don't you, you wicked, bad girl." Then Philomena slipped her hand between her captive lover's legs, and said, "My darling you are positively dripping. Shall I give you a little tap on these wonderful buns?" Without waiting for a reply she brought the silver brush singing down on the prone buttocks. Philomena's free hand had gripped the lips of Ursula's pussy and tugged gently, then a bit harder, as the brush came down with increasing force. She began to tickle the twitching clit and to spank the woman simultaneously. Ursula's buttocks were now a bright shade of red, and she wriggled with glee on Philomena's lap.

"That's it, my girl. Oh my...my darling, you are going to make me come. Oh yes." And Ursula let out a wail of satisfaction as the brush slapped the ripe flesh of her ass one last time.

Now spent, both women fell against the pillows. After some moments Philomena sat up, her lips compressed into a smile. "Come along, naughty Ursula. If you are still wanting, I am sure with some...ah...coercion you can have our new girl kneeling at your feet begging to be allowed to please you with her sprightly little tongue. I know you do so love to initiate the devotees this way, tears streaming down their country-fresh cheeks."

Ursula laughed heartily at the thought. "I do hope she will be one of the girls we will send on to the Isle of Man later this year. Remember that young thing, Catherine, whom I picked up in the very same pub last month?"

"How could I forget. Although she was a willing devotee at the beginning, that private spectacle you staged for the visiting priestess from the Isle..."

Again Ursula laughed. "I do suppose straddling that young buck from the Isle, and entertaining another pair of fine young devotees with her mouth and her bottom was quite too much for her inexperience. Although later she said she liked it so. What a pity she is too plain to send to the Festival this year. If this Brigeen shows promise, Catherine can teach her the entire repertoire she has mastered so far."

"Does Brigeen strike you as grateful to be here? After all, being taken from potatoes, boiled cabbage and buttermilk must come as a great shock to her."

"I think the luxury and pleasure here, in comparison to the the harsh life of the country, will make her all the more an apt pupil."

"This is good news. I do so want to make a good showing of girls this year."

The two women proceeded to dress carefully and slowly, until Philomena slapped her forehead and cried, "Ursula, how do you want to taste for the new girl? The conceited minx, Bernadette, is especialy fond of the taste of fennel, so fennel should be good enough for the maid from the boreens, I imagine."

"What an excellent idea, Philomena. How clever you are to remember. Do you still remember the names of every last one of the herbs and natural substances suitable for using as a douche?" Ursula busied herself with the phial of fennel essence.

"There are eleven. Let me think—fennel, fit root, slippery elm, gum arabica, white pond lily, marsh mallow, wild alum root, uva ursi, fenugreek, barberry bark and...the last I forget." Philomena concluded her litany ruefully.

"I will never forget you telling the novice devotees to use the natural secretions of their cunnies as a scent. What was it you told them?"

"Simply that a rub behind the ears and on the

34

throat works as well as any subtle and mischievous perfume. What's more, it costs nothing at all compared to all those fancy perfumes. It's something I learned on my first trip to the festival on the Isle. It is a powerful aphrpodisiac.

"Unfortunately, one strapping big girl from Longford went around smelling like the Liffey at low tide before I taught her that moderation in all things is a virtue in itself, even if conventional worship and austerity are not part of our particular order."

The two women laughed conspiratorially about this fact. At last, dressed and composed, the pair descended the carved oak staircase to the parlor. Awaiting them were Bernadette and the plump girl known as Loretta. Brigeen was sitting at their feet as she had been told to do.

"Has Brigeen been washed thoroughly, Bernadette?" whispered Ursula.

"Inside and out," replied the girl in a low giggle. "She needed some persuasion to take the enema nozzle, but Loretta held her securely while I did the necessary. The water was hardly hot, but she wailed like a banshee all the same."

"That will do, Bernadette. Has Loretta got everything she needs?"

"Begod, I have the lot," murmured Loretta.

The four stood back and regarded Brigeen. Each of them studied her dispassionately. Brigeen turned her pale face towards Ursula, the oldest of the group.

"You have nothing to fear, child. Look at me; you know what obedience means, I hope?"

"I think so, madam." Her voice sounded subdued and hesitant.

"Call me Ursula, love," said the older woman.

Brigeen looked around the warm room. It was truly the most opulent place she had ever been in.

The waning light illuminated the tall windows that held stained glass patterned into Celtic braids and strange runes that she had not noticed until now. They seemed slightly ominous. In the corner of the room stood what seemed to be a pagan altar. It had an ornately carved marble base. The surface was decorated with leaves, burning candles, and what seemed like bones. But she couldn't be sure. There was a plate of fresh fruit, and a loaf of bread. A rich carpet extended from this queer altar to the center of the room. It was on this that Brigeen, barefoot, stood.

"You have been chosen by Ursula to be instructed in the way of the Old Religion—The cult of the Goddess and her consort, the Horned God. You are not required to take the vows for another week, Brigeen," said Philomena. "Tonight will decide you, and I might add, decide us as well. It is a great honor to be selected. How thoroughly have you learned your lessons?"

"As thoroughly as I could, Sister Philomena," replied Brigeen confidently. She felt warm and dizzy. The events of the past few hours, so many moments of delight, had convinced her that she would stay in the company of these wonderful creatures and learn more of what they were about. She had been reassured by the sparkling character of Bernadette that only more pleasure was to come her way. And perhaps she would learn more of the "dark habits" her mother had always so fearfully made reference to. She had never really known what Mother meant by the dark way, but she had a feeling she was going to find out. It all felt deliciously sacrilegious, and the idea made her flush even more.

"To whom is your maidenhead consecrated, Brigeen?" asked Ursula quietly.

"To the Isle of Man, to the Great Goddess and her Mercurial Heralds of the Old Religion." Brigeen did not know what this meant, but she had been instructed by Bernadette to reply as much.

"And your vagina is consecrated..." prompted Philomena, her eyes sparkling.

"My vagina is consecrated and sacred. Only those blessed of the Holy Isle and the initiated are to know me as a woman."

"Not withstanding this," continued Bernadette, who had moved closer to Brigeen.

"Not withstanding this, my mouth, my hands, my breasts and my tightest aperture may be employed to enrich our Order in all matters spiritual and temporal."

"You have taught her well, Bernadette," observed Ursula approvingly. "Now, my dear Brigeen, adopt the posture Bernadette has shown you."

With only the slightest shudder of hesitation, Brigeen knelt and then leaned forward facing the altar. At a nod from Ursula, Bernadette slowly lifted Brigeen's coarse blue-grey schoolgirl skirt until the hem was around her waist.

"Her bottom is beautifully curved, a perfect hemisphere," breathed Philomena in Ursula's ear.

"Prepare yourself, my pupil in the way of the Goddess," intoned Ursula. "Loretta, a dozen light strokes, I think."

With a satisfied grunt, the plump girl produced a thin Malacca cane with a silver and ivory handle. She shuffled carefully forward until she stood beside the bare buttocks of the trembling girl kneeling in supplication before the altar and its gleaming candles.

"Begin when I clap my hands, Loretta. Brigeen, you are to recite the sacred utterances. The essential purpose of this beating is to stir the blood, make it quicken. Call out clearly while you are being caned. It is the vibration of your voice that evokes the passions of the Goddess. Do you understand?"

Her teeth chattering, Brigeen nodded. Ursula, her face gleeful, stood back and clapped her hands. The thin cane whipped through the air and made contact with the soft flesh.

"I-o-evoe-e! Ahh!" Brigeen was having difficulty making the strange noises as the rigid ritual cane came thrashing down on her soft buttocks. "We invoke...oh...thee, Queen of Queens. Oh...Aradia! Aradia! Ah..." The cane came whistling down again. "Ooo! Come to us in all our...ah!" Brigeen eyes were welling up with tears as the cane came down once again. "Ah...in all our dreams. Perfect love and Perfect...Ah...Oh...Perfect trust. Aradia! Aradia! Less would turn...Oh...All into...Oh...dust..." Brigeen was so frightened and moved by the strange predicament in which she found herself, that the feeling of the cane, and the moments between lashes, were beginning to become quite pleasurable. The sound of her own voice was mysteriously husky, transported. "Upwards on and...oh...oh...and on. Aradia! Aradia! Till...oooooh...our souls with thee are...one. Ah...Aradia!"

And with that, the cane ceased to cut through the air and did not crash down on her poor ass again. Brigeen felt tears streaking her face. The cheeks of her bottom were stinging, yet there was a warm sense of relief, almost pleasurable because compared to the harsh sting of the ivory staff, this was bliss. The words she had uttered had come out of a part of her that she did not know existed. And then there was that tingling sensation between her white, young thighs.

Loretta, visibly disappointed that she had been

permitted so little, sniffed and laid the cane aside with a shrug after the twelfth stroke.

Ursula and Philomena had begun toying with one another's breasts as the girl had uttered the sacred recitation. They were so moved by the sight of the virginal ass turning wine red with the beating, that they had fallen into each other's arms and lost themselves in lascivious kisses.

Bernadette could be seen lying back on some cushions, her thin legs sprawled apart. She was mesmerized by the sight of Brigeen's spanking, and could not help but tickle her own little pink cunt while the magic words were being uttered by this beautiful banshee. The recitation always elicited such an erotic response from her.

Brigeen looked up from her position and waited quietly for the women to take notice of her. She was too scared to interrupt the playful interludes of the women. At last Ursula wrenched her attention away from the wicked lips of Philomena.

"Brigeen, stop your recitation and pay attention to what I am now saying."

"Yes, Ursula," mewed Brigeen, soft tears pearling on her cheeks.

"You understand the meaning of obedience a little better now, I trust?" enquired the older woman archly. Without waiting for an answer, she turned to Loretta and murmured something Brigeen was unable to hear.

"The smaller one, I suppose?" responded the plump girl glumly.

"Of course. Not everyone has your capacity, you mare. You have the chism ready?"

A small chalice was produced from its place of concealment on the altar. Loretta's porcine hands laid it reverently before the stand, inches from Brigeen's nose. Philomena, determined to add a note of dispatch to the proceedings, knelt before Brigeen and opened her hand slowly to reveal a carved wooden object at which the girl stared incredulously.

"A Little Green Man from our sisters on the Isle, my dear. It will be thoroughly lubricated before it enters your pretty bottom, never fear. Once you have become accustomed to the sensation, you will be ready for the godemiche, another ritual object of pleasure from the rocky shores of the Isle. Don't fret, my girl. Bernadette and Loretta were once initiated as you are now." Philomena stood up and beckoned Bernadette to her side.

"Make the shaft thoroughly slippery, Bernadette. Let Brigeen watch."

Bernadette seized the contrivance from Philomena's grasp and held it in front of Brigeen's wide brown eyes. On a sudden impulse, she adjusted her grip and touched the bulbous head to her friend's lips, making Brigeen start with surprise.

"A devotee knows how to suck a cock as well as how to suffer herself to be buggered," she breathed. "Now, watch carefully."

Intrigued as much as appalled, Brigeen stared wide-eyed at the girl as she brought the oblong object to her own mouth. Her thin little tongue darted around the tip, and there she played her mouth over the smooth green marble. Then suddenly she slipped the strange thing all the way into her mouth. Her eyes were shining and a small growl erupted from her thin throat. Brigeen was entranced. Bernadette sucked the thing as though it were candy, so great seemed her delight at having this marble phallus in her mouth. And as quickly as she had popped the shaft in her pretty mouth, she withdrew it. With slim fingers, she immersed the slender shaft of the unthinkable object in the consecrated oil filling the

40

chalice. Held aloft before her eyes, the dark shaft glistened and shone in the chapel's light.

"You see, all you have had in your arse up till now has been my finger once or twice," whispered Bernadette. "This will really fill you up, believe me. Be brave and relax. Try not to howl out loud for a good minute or two. After that you will find the sensation surprisingly agreeable. Wait and see."

She massaged the oil diligently, lovingly into the shaft.

The voice of Ursula broke the silence.

"Very well, Bernadette. You may usurp Sister Loretta's prerogative in this instance; ours is not a religion in which cruelty is an end in itself. Not for us the ritual flagellations in stone-floored convents beneath the grey Donegal skies! Loretta, assist Bernadette."

With visible ill grace, the plump girl knelt and eased Brigeen's white buttocks asunder none-too-gently. Her ministrations exposed the deep cleft between the cheeks and—at last—the tiny knot of the girl's narrowest portal of love.

"Oh, Bernadette, I'm frightened," wailed Brigeen.

"Hush, silly," replied Bernadette briskly, reaching for the chalice and the carved marble curiosity half-submerged within it.

To Brigeen's surprise and relief, Loretta relaxed her grip long enough to enable her to ease her knees further assunder. The plump girl's nearer hand curled beneath her thigh. She gasped aloud as a fat little finger caressed the curls on her mons veneris before unerringly finding the tiny pink ridge.

To the watchful eyes of the onlookers, Brigeen's fleshy knot began to pulse in rhythm with the restrained and invisible stroking of Loretta's fingers. Loretta's smoldering eyes met Bernadette's and the younger girl grinned wickedly.

When a soft finger touched her, Brigeen knew it could only be Bernadette's, it was so gentle, so subtle, so loving. She made herself relax. The warm, greased knob at the tip of the object replaced the questing finger. Brigeen, by now confident that Bernadette would do all in her power to avoid causing her the least unnecessary pain, shuddered and sighed.

For an instant or two Bernadette made no progress. Then, miraculously, the tiny aperture pouted and yielded.

"Ooooooh," moaned Brigeen, uncertain as to whether she was feeling pain or exquisite delight. Little by little, the bulbous head at the tip of the shaft slid further into the nervous and apprehensive girl's rectum.

"Oh, Jesus Christ," gasped Brigeen, feeling every millemeter of the thing as it made steady progress into her. As if in reply, the steady strokes of Loretta's hidden finger quickened their pace.

"There, my darling, it's in all the way. Now relax and enjoy it." Bernadette's dulcet tones seemed to be coming from very far away. The shaft withdrew, returned, withdrew once more and returned a second time. Between her thighs, Loretta's fingers maintained their steady pace, pummeling, squeezing and stroking, exciting her immeasurably.

"Go on, go on...it's beautiful," Brigeen crooned, her head spinning.

Some distance beyond the trio, Ursula and Philomena stood watching, their arms hanging about one another lightly, fondling each other's nipples.

"Well, Ursula, now is as good a time as any. Give the little goddess something to do with her mouth other than sighing in appreciation."

Ursula smiled lasciviously at Philomena, saying, "Don't mind if I do!" She strode forward briskly until she stood at the foot of the altar, the hem of her long white robe all but brushing Brigeen's hair.

"You are demonstrating your obedience most impressively, my daughter," she said to the shuddering form at her feet. Brigeen stared up at the apparition before her, believing she had taken leave of her senses as the woman lowered herself carefully until a copse of dark curls was inches from Brigeen's open mouth.

"Bernadette has taught you how to lick, I believe?" The voice was soft, but the tone imperious.

"Yes...Sister...I am your slave to command."

"Then lick me, my daughter! Lick me hard and well until I tell you to stop!"

Brigeen was feeling the full pleasure of Loretta's teasing finger on her special node in the folds of her pink nether lips. It was heightened by the gentle thrusting motions of Bernadette's steady hands on her narrow anal opening. It all made her feel delightfully full. With every breath the pleasure was enhanced; she could feel the different sensations impacted by the heaving of her body.

She did not dare disobey a command from the woman now standing over her, and in a state of near delirium, she pressed her lips to the waiting cunt of Ursula. And oh! The taste was wonderful, musky, and tinged with the slight aroma of herbs. Brigeen could hear Ursula moan a little over her. Knowing that she was returning some of the pleasure she was receiving she set to lapping furiously at the wet lips of the woman, suckling like a hungry pup. She could hear cooing sounds around her, and in a haze of total gratification, she could feel the hips of Ursula gyrating against her eager tongue.

Brigeen could still feel Loretta's teasing fingers on her clitoris, made erect and pulsing from the caresses. Her body was thrust gently forward into Ursula's wet cunt by Bernadette's thrusts behind her. All her senses were titillated as she sucked harder and harder at the soft mouth of Ursula's dripping vagina. She could feel Ursula's strong hands pressing the back of her head, forcing her to press her probing, flicking tongue deeper and deeper into the hot recess of the older woman's cunt.

The pleasure from Loretta's fingers and the excitation of her virgin anus by the steady hands of Bernadette were so intense that Brigeen was making muffled moaning sounds into the open crevice of Ursula's spread legs.

The vibrations of the young girl's voice created a tingling sensation in Ursula, and she pressed Brigeen's head more firmly into her wildly throbbing pussy. As she did this, Brigeen's body began to convulse in wracking spasms of ecstasy. The sight of the young girl coming so forcefully beneath her made Ursula writhe in pleasure, clutching her own tits in her hands, and screaming out as she came into Brigeen's still sucking mouth.

There were more screams and sighs, and then in total fear and ecstasy, Brigeen lost consciousness.

-3-

They stepped out briskly—Brigeen and Bernadette—out of the imposing gates, under the railway arch, past the freighters at the dock, past the coal and the timber yards. Brigeen adjusted her new wool cape furtively. Her head felt distinctly odd now that her hair had been restyled and fell free about her shoulders in loose curls.

"Well now that we are both initiates, how does it feel?" enquired Bernadette solicitously.

"Odd, I suppose. To think that merely weeks ago I was going to be sent to a convent where I would have been forced to go through all the mumbo-jumbo of prostrating myself, taking ridiculous vows that I never really believed, and worse yet, being shorn like a country ewe. I feel so fortunate, so special being singled out by Ursula to come to know the secrets of the Old Religion. It seems that I was destined to it." She grasped Bernadette's arm a little more snugly.

"Oh, you were. Sister Ursula has the second sight. She always knows a devotee when she sees her, even

46

if the chosen doesn't know it at first. She is quick to initiate them."

"I have to admit, the first few days of hobbling around with the Sacred Green Man in my bottom made me wonder if I were a suitable candidate. But after a little time, it was almost quite pleasurable."

"A hallowed device, that Green Man. It seems that it was much in vogue in Persia long before Christianity was ever thought of. Some traveller brought the curiosity to the Isle and it was made a ritual object of the Horned God. This is what Ursula has told me. The tapered ceramic cone the Persians call the 'golule' stops one's sphincter muscle from being hurt or weakened when one is being fucked up the arse. After a while it no longer becomes necessary to use it. I wonder whether Persian dancing-boys keep them in place while they are actually dancing as we do, or whether they are removed as the curtain goes up."

They were ascending a steep hill towards one of the better parts of town on their way to what Bernadette had merrily called an assignation with a prosperous citizen. He was also a secret initiate, and was known for his generous contributions to Ursula's house, which helped keep the girls in clothes and food.

"I hate to confess it, but I feel unaccountably nervous," muttered Brigeen to her companion. Bernadette laughed lightly, aware that the pair were on public display.

"Oh, you mean the first time you will have to perform outside the safety of the house, the temple? Listen, all will pass fair and easy, to be sure. The pair of us suck his cock first, then I go on all fours and let myself be buggered by his consecrated prick while you watch. Perhaps Mr. O'Hara would be pleased if I

47

were to lap your delicious cunny while he takes me from behind. I know you wouldn't mind that too much, would you love?"

The two girls laughed conspiratorially. "It is the least we can do for so kind a Herald of our Order. Perhaps if he's pleased he'll give us a couple of bottles of Jamesons of Bushmills. It seems simply ages since I last drank decent whiskey."

"Bernadette, what's this devotee, O'Hara like?"

"He washes thoroughly before I kneel and suck him, which is a point in his favour. It is a practice of the Old Ways, but many forget, or are negligent about it. As to what he is really like, I still know surprisingly little about him. As you already gathered he is one of those quintessentially Irish self-made men so aptly described as gombeens. He was initiated into the Old Ways by his nurse, and because he was so well received on the Isle of Man by the Priestess, he has lead a blessed life hence. I am told he was sent to the Winter Equinox when he was barely fifteen, which says something about his prowess. It seems because he had managed to corner some of the Mysterious Powers, he had made himself quite successful. Every one who comes into the knowing is free to use the gifts of magic to his own ends. If perchance it is Black Magic, one simply has to be willing to pay the price of retribution. But O'Hara seems to have just wanted a little stash of wealth, which he secured without too many devious tricks of the Old Way. He takes care of us quite well, which is a sort of payback for his success.

"That's his house ahead of us now. Whatever else you do, Brigeen, conceal the contempt you feel for any ghastly religious iconography occupying every wall, shelf and windowsill in the house. It is to shield his true beliefs, and to deflect the curiosity of unwanted parties. He holds it in contempt as well, and to point it out would anger him. The main thing is to serve our brother and see that his thirsts are well quenched. It is our duty to the Goddess."

The house—tall, ivy-clad and handsomely proportioned—loomed before them. A maid opened the front door and curtsied. Bernadette made the protective sign of the Mano Fica over the girl's head and then she and Brigeen waited in the parlor while the girl scurried off in search of her master, a pretty sight in her black and white maid's uniform.

"It was all I could do to stop myself patting the sweet girl's pretty arse, Brigeen," giggled Bernadette. "Could you imagine her reaction? She is terrified of all of us from Ursula's. She'd probably be beside herself with arousal and fear. After all, you are a peasant maid yourself, so you should know as well as I do what unexpected desires an Irish country girl is capable of feeling."

The maid returned and stammered a message to the effect that the girls were to follow her to the master's study. Brigeen gazed at her compassionately, trying to imagine what her life was like. Bernadette's expressionless exterior, a cultivated specialty of hers, concealed her desire to rip every stitch of black and white off the girl, pin her to the carpet and give her what Philomena coarsely referred to as 'a thorough tonguing.'

Seamus O'Hara, who had been know as James before Irish independence, ushered the two young devotees into the high-ceilinged study with elaborate courtesy before quickly bolting the door behind him. He then silently exchanged the secret hand signal, the Mano Cornuta, the symbol of the Horned God, as Bernadette showed him the sign of the Great Goddess, the Mano in Fica. With that done he embraced Bernadette warmly.

"For God's sake give us both a drink, James," said Bernadette unceremoniously once they were seated.

"A bit of the sacred wine? The same for the new initiate?"

"That will do perfectly," said Brigeen, blushing furiously.

"I hope you're ready for a perfectly wonderful afternoon of worship, my lord. Today you get a two-girl lick before you enjoy my willing little asshole." She laughed softly, and then went on to explain that although Brigeen had been initiated, she had yet to be taken to the Higher Herald, and was still quite inexperienced in the pleasures of the Old Way.

"So her lovely derriere is still forbidden, I presume," sighed their host as he handed them each a large silver chalice of sweet red wine.

"Exactly," rejoined Bernadette, gulping hers eagerly. "Well, how is business? Have you made any of your friends in the government award you any new contracts?"

"Ah yes, the magic is working splendidly this year despite those vermin Republicans and the powerful spells and gold of the Russians that back them. I have still been able to carry on a booming business."

"The priest and the tyrant are ever to be found hand in hand, as Herodotus said," replied Bernadette softly, refilling her cup without waiting to be invited.

On a sudden roguish whim, the potent wine flushing her creamy complexion, Brigeen slipped to her knees and crept over to where James O'Hara sprawled in a comfortable leather armchair, his large muscular frame filling it completely. Brigeen was pleased to find him not unattractive.

"Well, James, do I have your permission to begin?" she enquired, her head cocked coyly to one side. Her lovely hair fell in ringlets around her rosy face. Her eyes gleamed mischievously.

"Let Brigeen try worshipping your cock on her own for a while, James," Bernadette called encouragingly. "She has never tasted one before. Or seen a real one for that matter. Tell her what to do; she's a willing girl and most eager to please."

Her fingers trembling with anticipation, Brigeen fumbled with a succession of stiff trouser buttons, the flap of O'Hara's flannel drawers, and a striped linen shirttail before she located the soft organ she sought. In disrobing him, Brigeen noticed a tiny facsimile of the green marble godemiche that had titillated and tortured her narrow rear entrance, hanging from a leather thong around James' neck. The sight of this inflamed her loins, and her hands quickly reached down and took the soft cock in her hands.

Her eyes were staring, as she brought it into the light of day, wondering at it as it began to turn slightly more red and large at her touch. It thobbed in semi-tumescent anticipation of what was to come.

"It's lovely," she breathed, before inclining her head to kiss it lightly.

"Take it in your mouth, young one," James urged. Brigeen, less apprehensive and by now thoroughly enjoying herself, grinned contentedly and opened her mouth to engulf the plum-colored glans-penis, holding the shaft between her forefinger and thumb.

"Good girl. Use your tongue the way I showed you with the godemiche. Remember, we are in no hurry," crooned Bernadette from her vantage point a few feet away.

Brigeen could hardly hear her, so absobed was she by the wondrously excitable penis that leapt to the

51

flick of her tongue. She slowly slid the growing member into her open mouth.

"Oh, great goddess, it is the mouth of a nymph you have," moaned O'Hara.

"Use your tongue softly and very gently, just enough for James to feel it," breathed Bernadette who had silently crossed the room and was kneeling next to the older girl as she gently suckled the stirring cock. Slowly, Bernadette began to unbutton Brigeen's dress. Brigeen sighed with delight at the soft touch of Bernadette's hand upon her. Soon she was naked to the waist, Bernadette's active little hands dancing all over her bare flesh.

"Put your hands on her tits, James. You will find them very much to your liking." And she gathered the full flesh there, offering them to male hands.

Seamus O'Hara needed no further urging. His strong, coarse hands cupped Brigeen's breasts the moment Bernadette presented them thus. Brigeen wiggled and squirmed as his rough palms excited her strawberry pink nipples.

"You like that, my little goddess?" gasped O'Hara, his hips rotating uncontrollably in his armchair as Brigeen energetically applied her inexperienced fingers, lips and tongue.

"O yes, yes I do. Be rougher. Squeeze them. I do love it so!" exclaimed Brigeen, briefly raising her pretty face, pink with her excited efforts.

"Now let me share your feast, my pet," murmured Bernadette, nudging Brigeen a little to the side.

O'Hara groaned and jerked his hips more violently as the two girls' tongues worked simultaneously over his rigid member. Bernadette snuck little licks at Brigeen's roving tongue, and the kisses were returned. The girls took turns taking him all the way in their mouths. While one sucked deeply, the other flicked little nips and kisses around his balls.

Bernadette was aware that O'Hara's climax was almost at hand. His ass was lifting off the leather couch and he was making deep, rasping moans.

"Let me take his cream in my mouth, Brigeen. Then both of us will share," said the younger girl firmly.

Willing enough to yield to her friend's expertise, Brigeen lifted her face and stared, engrossed, as O'Hara's hips bucked and jerked. Determined Bernadette, meanwhile, kept a firm grip and still a firmer mouth on his cock as successive jets of semen spattered against the back of her throat.

Her lips bubbling with froth, Bernadette turned to Brigeen an instant later. Their lips met and their tongues entwined in delicious lewdness. They pressed their lips together tightly, their mouths open, and shared the mystical male liquid. This wonderful substance, a very important part of the rituals, was said to be one of the most potent of aphrodisiacs. The two girls licked and sucked at each other's mouths, gulping down the precious essence. Bernadette moved her head back abruptly to allow a thick pearl of the milky white fluid to drip onto Brigeen's breasts.

"Your first bath of love, my dear," she uttered, quickly lapping up the little bit of cum. Then she lightly kissed both pert nipples. The trio, their passions spent for the moment, regarded each other with contented smiles.

"Did you find the flavor to your taste?" asked Bernadette wickedly as she wiped her glistening lips and chin on a handkerchief of pristine Irish linen thoughtfully provided by their host and spiritual brother.

"Sweet and salty at the same time. Odd, really," giggled Brigeen.

"James' magical essence always tastes very pleasant, I think," she said, smiling, glancing at the man who lay motionless on the couch.

"Is he alright, Bernadette?" enquired Brigeen, a note of anxiety in her soft voice. She got to her feet and moved closer to the flushed countenance that panted before her.

"Oh, but of course, silly goose," said Bernadette scoffingly, as she rose and poured some wine for the two of them. "He's well-trained in the Arts of Love. Just wait and see in ten minutes or so, when James gets his second wind. He wasn't a favourite on the Isle when he was a youth for no reason."

They sat close together on a low divan and sipped their wine thoughtfully, both happily flushed and gazing at the man they had so triumphantly fellated moments before. At last he let out a long sigh.

"Look, he is stirring. A drop of this wonderful wine will revive him, and then I shall require your close attention, my beloved initiate." With that Bernadette sidled over to where James, now recovered, sat bolt upright. She guided his large hand as he deftly unbuttoned her delicate lace camiknickers. When they were down around her knees, she purred as his fingers cupped her silken mound and rubbed the curls that formed the shape of a heart between her milky thighs.

Brigeen's ears reddened; she was aware of a stab of jealousy quite alien to her. Rooted to the spot, she felt rather than merely watched, as O'Hara's middle finger found its way between the succulent petals of Bernadette's moist rose and touched the tiny stamen

54

at its heart. Brigeen's loins ached. She felt a tugging down between her legs and her nipples became suddenly engorged.

Laughing, Bernadette pulled herself away from James and pirouetted vainly to the center of the room.

"With my corset and underthings, or without?" she pouted coquettishly.

"Without," her admirer growled.

Her innocent countenance made her all the more appealing as she trod lightly across the floor and permitted Brigeen to disrobe her until she stood naked, sleek as a forest wood nymph. Brigeen could not help but rub the tips of her aching nipples along the fine down of the younger girl's back. She nuzzled her neck. Brigeen's breathing became heavier, more rapid.

"Oh, you naughty thing," exclaimed Bernadette, shivering with glee. "There's enough time for that later! Now, do you have the phial of anointed oil from the Isle, Brigeen?" Her eyes were shining with anticipation.

Brigeen produced it immediately from within the folds of her skirts. She held it aloft, the thick green glass reflecting the light wondrously.

"Good, good, bring it here."

Obediently, Brigeen gulped the remaining drops of wine in her chalice and minced delicately across the room. Her eyes regarded those of the younger girl intently.

With a titter of amusement at Brigeen's rapt attention, so liberally bestowed upon her, Bernadette kneeled quickly and thrust her torso forward so that she squatted on all fours, just as Brigeen had in the altar room at Ursula's house. This was a position of respect and supplication to the Great Goddess.

"Watch me now. I will remain well bent over, my legs comfortably parted."

"What a perfect little apple she has, a treasure, and so deeply split. A truly divine spectacle," crooned O'Hara, his eyes widening with appreciation.

As she had been earlier instructed at great length, Brigeen knelt beside Bernadette's slender haunches and uncorked the phial. A sweet, pungent aroma filled the warm room. She spilled a few drops of the viscous fluid into her palms. Then, with slow deliberation, she worked the perfumed oil over her hands and blew delicately on her glistening fingers. The oil magically warmed to the soft wind from her lips. Brigeen then began to massage the tight little ass of Bernadette, who mewed her delightful response. Bernadette's flesh turned immediately more pink, as the mildly warm oil was worked over her spread cheeks. Then Brigeen got a mischievous glimmer in her eye, and began to tease the puckered little pink rose of Bernadette's anus.

"OH! OH! Don't tease me, girl! Oh, that's it! Your finger! Ah! It is slipping so nicely inside, right in my bottom! Watch us James! Oh!"

Her audience needed no encouragement, Brigeen reflected. O'Hara's eyes were huge as Brigeen's second finger slyly joined the first. Her hand moved in a gentle rhythm rotating slowly as the oil warmed and lubricated Bernadette's narrow passageway.

"Now put a little on his cock, you handmaiden of Venus," purred Bernadette from her crouched position.

Just as Bernadette had predicted, O'Hara's magnificent penis was every bit as swollen as it had been earlier. Brigeen eyed it hungrily. Impulsively, she stooped to kiss it, fondling and licking it like a woman possessed. Her fingers remained in the sweet little aperture between Bernadette's prone buttocks. Bernadette was gyrating her hips a little more wildly now. Then with solemn care, Brigeen removed her fingers from the deliciously lubricated asshole of Bernadette. She turned her full attention to O'Hara and began to massage the pungent warming oil into the throbbing purple head of his prick, the lance of the shaft and, with a deftly feminine touch, the tiny orifice at the head.

"Oh, there, girl. 'Tis enough of the petting. Put me in her sacred hole without a moment's delay!"

Brigeen said softly, "Let me draw you in, sir. Note her lovely bum so lasciviously and invitingly spread."

With a delicate, but sure grasp on O'Hara's engorged cock, she guided him to the little puckered mouth that opened and shut with anticipation. As a crowning touch, Brigeen reached down and oiled the lips of her accomplice's pouting slit.

Bernadette moaned softly as, tugged forward by Brigeen, the considerable plum of O'Hara's swollen manhood pressed against her well-oiled rosette. A snort of pleasure escaped him as he was urged inside. He pressed his solid hips forward and the glowing tip of his cock plunged roughly into the tight muscular ring that yielded to the remorseless thrust.

"Oh, Great Horned God, consort to the Queen, save me. It splits me. It is agony! Take it out!"

Brigeen smiled. For although her companion yelped and groaned, she could see her move quite gleefully over the thrusting cock. In fact, he had managed to push deep inside her, so that his dark oiled pubic hairs were brushing against the spread flesh of Bernadette's buttocks. He held her hips tightly, raising her rear off the floor to meet his energetic thrusts. Bernadette clawed the carpet, moaning for mercy. Then she slowly worked into an even, unfrenzied rhythm that matched James' drilling plunges into her asshole.

"Ah! What a feeling it is! Draw it out love, and push it right up again. Ah! Yes, that's it. Now more slowly, James, you pagan creature!"

"How tight you are, Bernadette. What a beauty!" That was all O'Hara could manage to say in between his excruciatingly delightful thrusts in and out of Bernadette's boyish butt.

"Am I warm and tight enough for you, love? Do you like buggering this little consecrated ass of mine?"

"There could be...no finer...in the...province of...Baile Atha...Cliath..." groaned O'Hara, as his excitement mounted.

Bernadette's little groans and rapid breathing prompted Brigeen to let her willing hand wander under her and cup the young girl's prominent mount with formerly innocent fingers that were now experienced in the arts of love. She caressed the creamy, stiffening ridge of pleasure. With her other hand she cupped the swelling balls of James. She gently followed the movements of the two, enhancing their pleasure, but not distracting from it.

"Ah...Great Mother! The pair of you have me in paradise. Faster now, James."

A thrill coursed through Brigeen as her lips met those of Bernadette's thrusting swain. Bernadette, almost swooning with so much loving attention, furiously pumped her narrow hips up and down to meet each stroke of James' quickening pace. They bucked, locked together, his hands gripping her hips so tightly. Brigeen was happily teasing Bernadette's clit, and toying with James' hanging scrotum. Suddenly, Seamus O'Hara let out a loud cry. At the same time, Bernadette threw her head back in the anguish of satiation, as his spasms of climax flooded through her. When he was finished, he pulled his cock from her. It came free with a wet, sucking sound.

"Your tongue, Brigeen. Use your tongue." Her voice was low, almost a growl.

Philomena's coaching had not been in vain, Brigeen thought suddenly. And, delighted to become part of the immediate activity, she thrust her head between the boyish cheeks of her younger friend and pressed her tongue deep into Bernadette's tightest orifice, rejoicing in the texture and taste.

"You two little sprites are a sight for the eyes as well as the cock!" declared O'Hara as he beheld Bernadette stretched, quivering, on the thick carpet while Brigeen's wandering tongue lapped at the traces of his foaming essence. He leaned forward and lifted Brigeen's skirt.

"I must get a glance at your soft white bum, too," he gasped. Brigeen gave a little start, but continued to service Bernadette's still-rotating behind. He pulled up the lustrous fabric and ran his rough hand over the globes of her perfect rear.

"It is customary to service all present at an afternoon's worship," O'Hara said with a smile on his lips. And so he reached under and began to tease the thoroughly moist pink lips of her pussy. His fingers gently tickled and probed, teasing the dark curls of hair that covered her there. O'Hara let out a grunt of satisfaction as he found the little hooded clitoris, stiff and quivering in response from his caresses.

Bernadette had craned her head around to witness James teasing her older girlfriend. She smiled to hear Brigeen's little coos of pleasure.

This is turning out quite wonderfully, she thought. She gracefully rolled over. Brigeen was momentarily confused, until Bernadette stroked her gleaming curls and said, "Lick me, my pet! Lick me as James sucks your little clitty now, girl."

Brigeen wordlessly pressed her head between Bernadette's tight thighs, as James' tongue began to flick rapidly over and around her dripping cleft. Bernadette arched her back and clutched the other girl's head, as Brigeen thrust her tongue inside her friend's pulsing cunt. James feverishly licked the new initiate's beguiling pussy from behind, his face buried between the lovely buttocks. They moved together in violent spasms.

"Oh! Darling girl, you are tormenting me—yes...Ah!" Bernadette shrieked, outthrusting her narrow hips right to Brigeen's mouth. Brigeen was making little muffled yelping sounds as James nipped at her throbbing pussy lips. His tongue penetrated inside and scoured the conch-like membranes. He brought her quickly and violently to a startling climax in tandem with Bernadette's cries of pleasure. Brigeen fell away, her mouth gleaming with the special juices of her younger friend. James had gotten to his feet and was licking his fingers as though he had just dined upon an incredible meal. Bernadette lay still and silent for a moment, then sat up on her elbows, her eyes shining.

"You are a wonderful little novice. A natural for the practices of the Old Way. Don't you think so, James?"

James just smacked his lips in a satiated response.

"Shall we have a drink, my friends?" Bernadette suggested happily.

The girls slowly made their way home. Bernadette carried a basket in which no fewer than four bottles of vintage wine were clanking together reassuringly. In an inner pocket she carried a cheque for fifty guineas made out to Ursula by Seamus O'Hara, Mercurial Herald of the Old Way.

"Well, am I to guess from your silence that you have learned something?" asked Bernadette, turning her head sharply. Her companion's silence vexed her and irritated her.

"Of course I have. Surely that much is obvious!" rejoined Brigeen. Softening immediately on seeing the hurt expression on her friend's young face, she added, "Watching you in action was more instructive than an afternoon of subjection to the godemiche wielded by Philomena or even, dare I say, Loretta."

At the mention of the plump young devotee's name, both burst out into laughter. Sister Loretta, as Brigeen knew all too well, liked nothing more than to use the Little Green Man, the long godemiche, the birch, and the thin Malacca cane until even the proudest devotee sobbed for mercy.

"That is good to hear," replied Bernadette, mollified. "By the way, I was asked by Ursula to judge your behavior attentively this afternoon. You will be delighted to hear that my report will be positively glowing in its praise." She smiled knowingly.

"What report? Why were you asked to judge my behaviour?" demanded Brigeen, alarmed.

Bernadette grinned even more broadly than before.

"Because you are to make a journey soon, my dear. And I have been chosen to accompany you."

"A journey?" Brigeen echoed, still at a loss to understand what Bernadette could mean.

"A journey to the Isle of Man, my dear. But first

61

we must be approved by the High Priestess on the mainland. It seems that we are going to take part in the Rite of Venus this year. Only after you have paid respects on the Isle are you a fully respected initiate in the arts of the Old Way!"

# -4-

The Mercurial Herald of the High Priestess leaned back and belched behind his napkin. His soft white hand lifted a bulbous brandy glass; his aquilline nose savoured the rich bouquet of the amber-dark liquid as it swirled enticingly before being tentatively sipped. An appreciative silence followed.

"As I was saying," he shortly resumed, "from earliest Neolithic times, the people of Europe and those parts of the British Isles not covered in ice venerated the Horned God, the Old God, Consort to the Goddess. A rather Dionysian figure by all accounts, he was. He provided harvests and bawling babies; a merry, rather hirsute deity who delighted in music and dancing and the pleasures of the flesh. A god of forest, pasture, river and flesh, if you like. A fecund provider as readily evoked through fornication as through prostration and prayer. A god much loved because he loved, putting pleasure far ahead of asceticism. His purpose was to serve the Mother, the Queen. A god, in short, to whom jealousy and vengeance were completely unknown."

"Hardly like the vindictive deity that so many fools think is lord of this land. Ah...they are so unaware of the truth, the Old Ways," ventured his hearer.

Phelim grinned lopsidedly and devoured half a dozen grapes before speaking again.

"Look what the early church, in its wisdom, managed to do to the Old God's and Goddess's festivals. His feast days were on April the thirteenth—Walpurgisnacht, February the second—Candalmas, the first of August—Lammas, and the last day in October—Hallowe'en. The feast they now call Christmas was originally a winter revelry of the Old God, as was Easter—a festival of new life and rebirth. Well into the morbidity of Christian times, folk traditions remember our own Green Man, yet he is relegated to the chicanery of a leprechaun. Ah...they are sorely misled. I do believe the old Gods and Goddesses are restless. The Festival of Venus this year should be particularly...fierce. I so look forward each year to this worship of the Great Goddess."

Phelim sighed and glanced out the tall window of his old manor. Soon, he hoped, very soon, his car would appear with its precious cargo. He grunted aloud with satisfaction and absent-mindedly permitted his hand to wander between his thighs.

"Ursula's young initiates should appreciate the lovely car you sent for them," the young male novice observed brightly.

The Mercurial Herald closed his eyes, savoring the delight he had felt on beholding his magnificent vehicle for the first time. It had been a gift from his cousin, a captain in the Chicago police. Built for a

65

prominent bootlegger. The cousin had offered the gangster the services of his spiritually powerful relative. Phelim had cast protective spells over the various houses of ill-repute that the gangster ran. The charms naturally worked, and the custom Packard had been a gift of thanks for the undisturbed continuation of the speakeasies and houses of pleasure. Phelim smirked at the wisdom of that gangster.

"So they should, the ignorant little country girls," Phelim replied at last. "Most of them have never ridden in anything grander than an asscart before taking the vows of the Old Way."

At last the Herald caught sight of the Packard advancing majestically up the gravelled drive. He was pleased to see the potential little priestesses arrive in such high style.

"Begob," he roared, "the new girl in the harem is here at last!" With a start, he hurled his powerful body to the window, his long white mane of hair flying about him.

"By the nipples of the Great Goddess herself, the new one is a lovely wee girl," announced the Herald, his blues eyes squinting hard out the Georgian windowpane.

"Remember, lord, that we are not allowed to deflower the young thing. She is to arrive on the Isle intact, as ordered by the High Priestess," the handsome young novice softly, but sternly reminded the older man.

"I'll fuck the wee thing senseless, I tell ye!" But Phelim, the Mercurial Herald, knew that he would truly suffer the wrath of the High Priestess herself if he did go against her express wishes. He had been ordered to inspect the girl and see if she was a proper devotee to represent the mainland. The thought of simply toying with the beautiful young creature made his sizeable cock strain at his trouser fly.

Brigeen and Bernadette descended daintily from the car, assisted by the chauffeur. Brigeen was about to stride forward but something in Bernadette's manner checked her.

"Stay where you are. Let him see you properly; I know he is watching," hissed Bernadette.

Emboldened, Brigeen smiled radiantly at the house and turned to her friend, a question on her lips.

"Are we to be fed first, I wonder? Or will we be inspected and pawed right away?"

"Hush, Brigeen. Even ivy has ears in these parts. Wait and see."

The front door opened.

"Is that the Herald?" asked Brigeen. She looked desperately relieved because the young man was quite handsome.

"No, goose. That's only a novice, like ourselves. You will probably get to know him soon enough, of that you can be sure. Follow me and be demure and polite."

The young man beckoned, and the two girls walked slowly across the gravel drive. Brigeen let herself be led by Bernadette. Up the steps. Over the threshold and through the paneled hallway. The smell of incense clung to the close air. There were strange scimitars, knives, and other odd objects affixed to the walls. The atmosphere was dense and mysterious.

"My lord, may I present Brigeen, a new member of our order." Bernadette's manner, Brigeen noted with an inner chuckle, was faultless. It was as though she were presiding over the opening of a temple.

"Brigeen, my dear," the Herald interrupted her thoughts loudly, "come and sit yourself down beside the fire."

67

Smiling sweetly, Brigeen did as she was told and looked around her. The place was comfortable. The chairs were deep and soft, the dark room regal yet somehow restrained. She looked up sharply; the Herald was speaking to her.

"Have you learned a lot from Bernadette, daughter?"

Brigeen immediately found herself speechless in front of this terrifyingly handsome older man. He seemed immense to her. He had silvery hair that fell in flowing waves around his square face. His perfectly manicured beard was groomed quite conspicuously into a point. His blue eyes were fierce and penetrating, and there was a lilt in his voice that was hypnotic to Brigeen.

"Well, my wee one. You need not be affrighted of me. Now why don't you two go on upstairs and make yourselves more comfortable. I shall be along shortly."

Without further ado, the girls rose, and once outside the study went scurrying upstairs. Bernadette led the way, and soon they found themselves inside an opulent bedroom. A huge mahogany four poster bed was the centerpiece of the lush room. It was covered with a deep brocade coverlet. There was a canopy over the bed, made of regal purple velvet. There were many strange objects in the room—crystals and bones and feathers and jars of curious powders and substances.

Brigeen gasped. It was truly magnificent. "Is it not wonderful, Bernadette?"

"Oh, yes. It is quite lovely in here."

Brigeen's eyes landed on a small sampler that rested on the wall at the head of the bed, incredulity writ on her features.

"A quote attributed to Queen Maeve," laughed

Bernadette. "The Celtic lettering is not easy to read, is it? Let me read it to you:

"'My husband must be free from cowardice, free from avarice and free from jealousy, for I am brave in battles and combats and it would be a discredit to my husband if I were braver than he. I am generous and a great giver of gifts and it would be a disgrace to my husband if he were less generous than I.

"'It would not suit me at all if he were jealous for I have never denied myself any man I desired and I never shall, whatever husband I have now or hereafter.'

"Rather lovely, don't you think?" Ursula gave it to Phelim years ago."

"Maeve was a pagan, was she not?" beamed Brigeen, quite taken with admiration for the quote.

"Why, certainly. Every intelligent man and woman in Ireland is a pagan at heart, whatever their public protestations might be. We are just lucky enough to be initiated into the subtlely of the secrets, and of course, the pleasures." Bernadette continued talking as she removed the last stitch of fabric from her lithe body.

"Shall I undress, too?"

"No, love, just stay as you are until Phelim gets here." As she spoke she went over to a tall armoire and took from its dim recesses a sumptuous garment at which Brigeen stared in puzzlement.

"My sacred robe. I keep it here for use when I bring a little joy into the Mercurial Herald's life. Listen, Brigeen, just wait for him to decide best how he will inspect you. Is your piece of sponge still in place?"

Blushing, Brigeen reached under the hem of her dress and ascertained that the shred of sponge, impregnated with olive oil, was indeed guarding the entrance to her womb, a humble Cerberus doggedly guarding the gateway.

"That delicious little spice-box of yours most assuredly will go untouched. It is the order of the High Priestess that we arrive virgins on the Isle. The sponge is just a precaution of Ursula's. She knows Phelim's wicked temper and passions better than anyone. Yet they all fear the High Priestess, and I shudder to think what would happen if Phelim were to disobey."

There was a sound of footsteps beyond the bedroom door and Brigeen shivered apprehensively despite the warmth of the fire that blazed in the hearth. A strong hand, bearing a huge ring with runes inscribed upon its enormous surface, turned the knob, and the Mercurial Herald, the favorite of the High Priestess herself, entered the room.

"Good girl, Bernadette. I see you have made yourself at home while waiting for the old fellow. Why don't ye warm my blood by doing some of the acrobatics first, before we begin the inspection of the fine new girl?"

He sat down, his sharp blue eyes dancing expectantly.

Bernadette directed a lewd wink at Brigeen and selected a spot on the floor. She found a piece of chalk and made a circle in the carpet. Then she sat down abruptly in the center of the circle, her sheer robes a shimmering sea of white folds about her. She gracefully parted the opening in front to reveal her boyish charms. It was obvious to Brigeen that she was enjoying herself.

Intrigued, Brigeen watched as Bernadette stretched out on the floor and drew her knees up to her chin. An instant later her legs were crossed behind her head and her pale arms were neatly pinning back her long thighs. A further effort and her lovely tuft of chestnut curls was brushing her forehead.

"A wee bit more, Bernadette," cried Phelim excitedly. "I can see that Ursula has taught you well, you little minx. Now, lick that pretty slit."

A sigh and a sudden wriggle was Bernadette's response. To Brigeen's astonishment, Bernadette had contrived to roll herself so tightly into a ball that now her pointed tongue was delicately lapping the fur-fringed slit Brigeen had come to love so much herself.

"That's right, flick your clit for me, girl!" breathed Phelim. Brigeen noticed that he had drawn his massive sword and was stroking it lightly to the rhythm of Bernadette's wondrous tongue lashing. Brigeen, earnest to make a good impression on so powerful a man, rose to her feet, never taking her eyes from the spectacle that Bernadette presented.

"Let me," Brigeen said softly, taking the Herald's enormous member in her own small hands.

Bernadette's body was already beginning to spasm with self-inflicted pleasure. Her wildly twisted body was covered with a fine sheen of perspiration as she continued to greedily tease and suck her own cunt.

"Oh, my lord, how beautiful," said Brigeen as she regarded Phelim's cock. It was much larger than that of James O'Hara's. She instinctively put her lips to the rising member. It was darkly veined and thick, and capped with a wide purpling bulb that filled her mouth.

Phelim closed his eyes for a moment, groaning deeply. Then he regarded Bernadette's quaking body, so close to climax.

"That's enough, Bernadette," barked the Herald suddenly. Bernadette, with amazing ease, uncurled her legs, and was instantly on her feet. She eased over to Brigeen who was kneeling before the man, her lips playfully darting around the head of his penis.

71

"Well, Brigeen. You certainly wasted no time, did you?" She ruffled the older girl's golden hair.

Brigeen made a muffled response. She was determined to do her best, and it seemed as though Phelim was liking it well enough. He reached out for Bernadette, and began to tease her budding breasts. She leaned forward to his touch, her nipples swelling. Brigeen continued to lick Phelim's cock hungrily, taking care to lave the underside of his shaft as well as the burning helmet while working his inflamed balls wih her agile hands. There was a look of genuine hunger in her half-closed eyes as she took the swelling shaft in and out of her mouth, her tongue continuing to tease the burning head of Phelim's cock.

"That's it, my girl," Phelim said in a low voice. "And you, my little minx," he said, regarding Bernadette, "come closer." He roughly tugged the smaller girl to him by the nipple that he had been teasing with his finger.

Bernadette squealed with glee, and climbing over Brigeen's bobbing head, she nestled closer to his chest. She rubbed her naked torso against the greying fur of his. Phelim's hands roved her body mercilessly. He toyed with her little strawberry nipples, ran a rough hand over those boyish buttocks, and at last a hand found the incredibly moist patch of flesh between her tight little thighs.

"Now, Phelim," Bernadette warned breathily, "you can touch, but that is all." It seemed to be as much an appeal to her own lascivious feelings as it was to his.

Brigeen was softly moaning with pleasure as she at last took the whole of the man's engorged penis into her willing throat.

Bernadette placed a knee on either armrest of the

72

chair that Phelim was slumped in, his hips rising and falling ever so slightly to meet the kiss of Brigeen's angelic mouth. Bernadette was straddled over him, but not touching him. Her gleaming pussy was thrust forward. She was taking obvious pleasure in displaying her nymph-like body to the powerful Mercurial Herald. He was not at all displeased to be confronted with the damp and quivering body of the girl, not to mention the lovely initiate who was so gifted with her lips and tongue.

He thrust his hand out and began to toy with the dripping lips of Bernadette's moss-fringed mound. She arched her back in appreciation of his touch. His fingers spread the delicate little folds of flesh there and began to probe with short thrusting motions. Meanwhile, Brigeen had started to quicken her pace on his cock. Her head was bobbing up and down, while Phelim's hips rocked up to meet her mouth. With every buck of his hips, his fingers probed more deeply into Bernadette's virginal cunt.

"Ah...My lord, that feels so..." Bernadette's small frame was gyrating in its precarious position kneeling over him on the armrests. "Careful sir Ohh! You know that we are...Ooooh! consecrated...to the Goddess. Ohh yes...Push it in, harder....NO!"

Bernadette suddenly regained control of herself as Phelim inserted more than three fingers into her slippery cavern. She was so desirous, but it was forbidden. It was law that she and Brigeen would be ritually deflowered on the Isle. But she wanted his fist inside her. Her body ached for it.

"Stop, Brigeen," Bernadette ordered, jumping up from her position. But Brigeen had lost herself in a frenzy of activity. Bernadette leaned down and lightly tugged the girl's hair in order to make her stop.

"You are right, my love," sighed Phelim, his eyes

73

dancing with a mischievous glint. "I would have taken your maidenhead then and there. You are a most devoted initiate. It seems that I have broken a sacred trust..."

Bernadette immediately understood the intent of Phelim. She had regained a sense of surety knowing that their virginity, hers and Brigeen's, was not in danger. Even in the wild pleasures of which they would partake together, Phelim would observe the law. But he was asking to be punished.

"Yes, you did breach the sacred trust. Sister Ursula sent us to you, trusting that we would return unblemished and unstained."

Bernadette now paused dramatically, and standing naked beside Brigeen, who was a bit confused by this laughing exchange between the two, threw her arm around the older girl. Regarding Phelim, she said at last, "So, it seems, my lord, that you will have to be punished." Her eyes gleamed with vicious delight.

"I do think you're right, little sister," Phelim smiled back at the forward young girl.

Bernadette turned and went to the huge armoire, and hunting in the depths, withdrew a bundle of slender birch twigs.

"I think I'll give Brigeen the honor of belaboring your holy backside," she said, brandishing the long reeds. "I believe she will be able to provide sufficient punishment for your near transgression. Now onto the bed with you, my holy, naughty one."

The Herald's immediate compliance with this order from the young girl gave Brigeen confidence. For a moment she had not fully understood the conversation between the two, but because they both seemed to be smiling with anticipation, Brigeen felt that whatever was to happen was in the name of pleasure.

74

Snorting with ill-concealed merriment, Bernadette arranged the man to her liking.

"You'll be pleasuring me with your wicked little tongue in order to soothe some of the discomfort of the 'punishment', I trust," said Phelim to Bernadette as she leaned over him.

"As it pleases you." And with that she gave his muscular ass a heavy love slap.

She went to Brigeen and pressed the birch into Brigeen's hand. "Get ready, lord, this strapping coleen is about to tickle you." And then, pleased with the tableau she had set up, Bernadette stationed herself facing the kneeling man.

Still somewhat in awe of the Mercurial Herald, Brigeen raised the birch lightly and let it fall across the crouching shaman's raised buttocks.

"Hit him, you goose!" shrieked Bernadette, visibly annoyed to see her pupil so half-hearted at so crucial a moment.

Brigeen took a deep breath, and with a mighty effort of will, she raised her arm to its furthest extent and lashed out with a fury. To her horror, mixed with a strange sense of satisfaction, she found that a trace of thin red stripes now marked the handsome buttocks before her.

"Good girl!" Bernadette shouted. "Now! Do it again!"

Well enough, thought Brigeen. If this is what is required, I can administer as much of this as his holiness can take! And thoroughly warming to her task, she lashed out a second time, then a third, then a fourth. She was so focused on her task, that only after several more lashings did she see that Bernadette had plunged her head between the thighs of Phelim. Brigeen felt a warm pleasure course through her body as she observed her friend delicately lapping the raised cock of the herald.

Phelim was squirming with delight. It occurred to Brigeen that the touch of the birch intensified his pleasure, a sensation she had come to know at Ursula's house. She resumed the thrashing. She raised and lowered her arm repeatedly, making sure her strokes matched with the rise and fall of Bernadette's bobbing head. Phelim was crying out in hoarse yelps of pleasure.

When Brigeen noticed that the thrusting buttocks before her were criss-crossed with red marks, she heard Bernadette say in a low heavy voice, "Just a wee bit more, six or eight strokes, and my lord will be entering the gates of paradise." And with that her face disappeared between the shaking thighs of Phelim, who immediately pressed her head down violently over his engorged cock.

Panting with her effort, her pussy dripping from so much excitement, Brigeen raised the reeds and brought them crashing down on Phelim's ass. She could hear his cries of pain and ecstasy, and as if from far away she could hear her own voice crying out with passion. She watched as Phelim's strong hands pulled at Bernadette's hair, as his strong pelvis thrust his huge member deep into her throat. The birch rods came down again and again, and then she saw Phelim rise up, clutching Bernadette with him. She flicked one last stroke on his raw flesh as he shot his powerful fountain into the back of Bernadette's throat.

When they were finished the girls tended to the Mercurial Herald's welted ass. Bernadette went to a shelf that held many jars of powders and salves. She expertly selected a soothing ointment. She immediately set about applying the magical rub to the aching flesh of Phelim's red bum.

"You did wonderfully," Bernadette whispered to

76

Brigeen. Phelim had fallen into a post-coital doze, and she was sure that he could not hear them.

Brigeen was flushed from effort. She was also a little frustrated, because her cunny was still aching and she was wishing that she had had the pleasure of Phelim's hand there. She was wildly attracted to this mysterious older man. At the same time she was ashamed of her own feelings, and attempted to hide them.

"'Twas nothing at all." And then, after a thoughtful pause, she said, "Bernadette, do let me apply that salve to his poor bum. It was I, after all, who inflicted the wounds."

Bernadette smiled knowingly and handed her the jar of liniment.

"I do believe you're smitten, my little love."

Brigeen simply blushed and began to lightly rub the cream into Phelim's flesh.

"Well," Bernadette smiled at her friend, "perhaps he will be your choice for defloration at the festival."

Brigeen brightened. "Do you think so?"

"One never knows. But Ursula will tell you all about it if you've passed the 'inspection' by Phelim. I should think we did fine."

Phelim was beginning to stir, and this silenced the girls' confidential conversation. He moaned sleepily and groped at his backside while Brigeen had continued to rub it with the healing salve. He grabbed her wrist harshly and tugged her around to his face. The two exchanged in silent stares. Brigeen felt chills run over her flesh.

Phelim said nothing, but continued to regard the pretty face of the girl. After some moments, he let go.

After the three had ritually bathed in warm, scented water, and shared a bottle of fine red wine, they descended the stairs together. Brigeen could not rid herself of the chilling sensation she had in Phelim's presence. Phelim made the secret sign at the door as the girls departed. He also gave Brigeen's breasts a stiff little pinch as they turned down the stairs to go.

The ride home to Ursula's was uneventful. Rain lashed against the Packard's window. Brigeen, lost in her own thoughts, stared at the green countryside through which the comfortable vehicle sped so effortlessly. At length she turned to her friend and spoke, her voice deliberately quiet so the driver might not overhear them.

"What was it that the Herald said to you as he handed us both into the car, Bernadette?"

Bernadette smiled knowingly before replying.

"Just as I expected, he said you were so pretty and I...I am too modest to say it easily—I am so talented that surely we will be favorites at the festival this year." She chuckled, delighting to behold the expression on Brigeen's face.

"Among so many other girls, Bernadette?"

Bernadette lit a pungent Turkish cigarette and grinned.

"We are to be queens. Queens!" exclaimed Brigeen, jubilation in her voice. Her eyes were bright with unfeigned excitement that Phelim had taken special notice of her beauty.

# -5-

March winds ruffled the blue surface of Loch Oughter. The willows were in bud, the finches and long-tailed tits busy in the hedges and woods. So unseasonably warm was the sun that the first red-gartered moorhens had begun to build their nests.

Such Arcadian scenes, though, were far from the minds of two young girls in Corderry House overlooking the chill waters of the loch.

Emerald, the last of a line of fading Anglo-Irish aristocracy, slid her hand between her companion's warm thighs and giggled.

"It's a pity we have to send you off to your family in Dublin, though I don't doubt there'll be enough of this for you in the city."

A woebegone face stared up at her for an instant, though a heartbeat later both girls dissolved into subdued laughter.

"Do it again, Emerald. Do it all over again."

Amused, and no less than excited, Emerald slid her hand into Peggy's crumpled housemaid's blouse and softly caressed her breast. She bent quickly and lifted it slightly to her teeth. The roseate nipple quivered erect in her mouth as her lips tugged delicately on the vulnerable soft flesh, harder and harder on the sensitive tissue.

"Don't stop, Emerald. Please don't stop!"

Encouraged, Emerald ran the tip of her tongue over the tiny jutting peak, swished it swiftly back and forth, the nipple trembling as her tongue softly circled it. She gently took it in her mouth and began to suck softly, pulling at the reddening aureole.

Abruptly she stopped and grinned, awaiting Peggy's reaction. A small, hesitant cry and a gasp escaped the younger girl's lips. Purring, Emerald rubbed her lips roughly against the pretty nipple, now glistening and slippery with her saliva; growling deep in her throat, she played delicately with it.

"Oh, how you tease me! It's unbearable. Oh, Emerald, don't stop!"

Emerald nipped with her teeth, released her prey and pounced again, surrounding and enveloping the stiff flesh with her teasing, tantalizing mouth. Again and again she darted her tongue over and around the bright bud, drawing it gently—then with mounting desire—between her moist lips.

"Ooooooh! Emerald, my darling," mewed the housemaid, staring up with wide eyes.

Suddenly, Emerald's caresses ceased. She pulled her taut body away and held herself poised over her companion, her strong hands pinning Peggy's wrists to the bed. Her victim writhed in agitation and excitement.

"You are not to touch me, Peggy," Emerald laughed, relishing the younger girl's discomfiture.

"You can look at me and feast your eyes on what you want, but you are not to touch me until I give my permission."

Triumphant, Emerald adjusted her position on the lace-covered bed and sprawled beside Peggy, smiling as she pressed the girl's wrist against the soft goose-down bolster at the head of the bed. Her free hand slowly groped along the length of the maid's trembling body, felt beneath the crumpled black skirt, slid over the stocking top and gave a determined pinch to the girl's warm thigh.

"For the love of God, put your fingers in my slit before I go mad altogether," whimpered Peggy, her eyes screwed fast shut and her voice breathless.

"All in due course, you wicked child," sniggered Emerald. Her hand rested lightly on the girl's mount of Venus before gliding lower. She twirled the damp hair there between her eager fingers. She pressed the hard nub and the soft flesh covering it.

"Ohhhh! You will drive me to distraction," moaned Peggy.

Emerald's fingers felt soft, enfolding flesh as her hand pressed gently between Peggy's thighs. Her thumb and forefinger tugged playfully at the full lips of the other girl's pussy. The maid's body writhed in ecstasy, oblivious to all but Emerald's hands and mouth.

"And now, my pretty Irish maid, I am going to undress you," she growled, "very slowly, just as I always do."

One by one, the items comprising Peggy's modest housemaid's uniform were discarded and thrown onto the elaborately patterned Persian carpet. There they lay incongruously entwined with Emerald's hunting skirt, tall boots, and the leather riding crop.

82

"Your tongue, Emerald. Please let me have your tongue," pleaded Peggy.

Her mistress surveyed the scene before her; this was a moment Emerald especially treasured, listening to Peggy plead to be brought to the heights of sensual pleasure.

"And where do you want my tongue, my wanton little slut?" Emerald smiled broadly.

"Oh, Emerald, you know where I want it. Don't make me say it. I feel so ashamed!"

"Tell me where you want my tongue, pretty miss," laughed Emerald, delighting in the picture Peggy presented. Small firm breasts, their nipples erect, a deliciously smooth cream-white stomach, and a trim garden of moist curls. A true Irish rose, Emerald thought.

"In my little puss, Emerald," whispered Peggy, reddening.

"Well, my wicked vixen, you must tell me what to do." Emerald knelt between the young girl's thighs and bowed, a naked priestess before a shrine.

"Lick me. Please lick me, Emerald," implored Peggy.

Feeling that she had teased Peggy sufficiently, Emerald squirmed lower until her long arms embraced Peggy's thighs and her tongue flicked lightly across the soft pink labia.

"Right inside," pleaded Peggy with a long sigh. Her arms, obedient to her mistress's commands until now, freed themselves from the bolster and her hands caressed Emerald's head.

Emerald inhaled deeply, savoring the warm and primitive scent of Peggy's slit before her tongue uncurled the tiny hood of flesh and teased the stiffening nub at the apex of Peggy's pinkness.

"Oh, oh yes. That's marvellous!" squealed

Peggy, pushing her loins with an involuntary shudder against the older girl's mouth.

"Be quiet, you silly ninny. My mother might hear you!" Emerald commanded sharply, her voice muffled. As though nothing had happened to disturb her concentration, she busied herself with her task once more, flicking her tongue this way and that. It slid craftily over the sopping lips of the other girl's cunt, teasing her until at last it entered the moist warmth of Peggy's nether mouth. Then as quickly as she had entered with her wet tongue, Emerald darted her it out again and sought the little swollen pearl of Peggy's clit. Peggy was making wordless sounds, her hips jutting forward to meet the tongue.

"Hush!" Emerald hissed again. She strengthened the grip of one hand on Peggy's hip, while the other tormented one nipple and then the other.

Peggy bit her lip in order to stifle the sounds that were coming from her throat; she could taste a little blood where the skin was broken. This seemed to heighten her pleasure and soon her body was writhing furiously, her back arched. Suddenly she shuddered. One climax after another crashed through her body as Emerald continued to suck hungrily at her cunt.

They lay together, warm and sweating in one another's arms. Peggy's sharp tongue slowly licked the pungent juices of her own passion from her mistress's face. Peggy then nuzzled her face into Emerald's warm armpit and twirled her tongue in the tangle of richly hued curls there, remembering that Emerald had not bathed since her return from the hunting field.

"How may I please you, Emerald, my darling?" she enquired timidly after some minutes had elapsed.

Emerald wrapped her long legs around Peggy's waist before making her decision. At last she rose and crossed the room, her naked body glowing with the flush of anticipation. She picked up the riding crop.

Peggy, reclining on one elbow amongst the pillows, gasped, "OH NO! No, Miss Emerald, not that, please not that..." her voice trailed away. The lascivious grin on the young girl's face belied her true emotions.

"Well, if you'd rather not please me...." Emerald paused, tapping the leather crop in her open palm.

"Oh, miss..." yelped Peggy, leaping from the bed, "anything you like. I just want to please you."

"In that case, bend over, girl," Emerald commanded imperiously.

Peggy complied immediately, kneeling on all fours and offering up her luscious white ass. Emerald then straddled the girl. She let her damp pussy hairs trail over the already quivering back of Peggy. She then took the small crop and began to lightly stroke the plump, pale flesh of Peggy's backside with it, teasing her. The light touch of the lethal little whip made Peggy squeal with fear and delight. Emerald now was letting the sweet lips of her dripping pussy graze the flesh of Peggy's back. As she was tickling herself there, she continued to rub the crop along the curve of the younger girl's bottom, and then allowed the stiff leather to slip into the spread crevice of her ass.

"Oh, miss, that feels so....oh!" Peggy gasped suddenly as Emerald pushed the tip nearer to the little rosebud anus.

"That's it, my girl," said Emerald throatily. "You shall be my horse. And I shall ride you." And with that she withdrew the probing crop and brought it down smartly on Peggy's creamy soft flesh. As the crop made contact, Peggy moaned, and Emerald sat more heavily on the girl's back. The full pink lips of her labia spread and she allowed the throbbing nob of her clit to touch the warm flesh of Peggy's back.

"Ah, yes, my pretty little pony, yes," crooned Emerald as she brought the crop down again behind her on the girl's exposed buttocks. She plunged her hips downward against the soft flesh again, and then again. She was moaning now, and her juices flowed so that she was sliding easily against the now-bucking body of Peggy. Emerald gathered a handful of Peggy's strawberry hair and, holding it like soft reins, began to rock violently back and forth.

Now Peggy was also moaning with mixed pleasure at the tingling sting of the leather crop on her ass and the glorious feeling of Emerald's dripping wet cunt rubbing back and forth on her bare flesh. She could not help but rock and buck like a wild horse, so great was her excitement. Her head arched back to keep Emerald from pulling so violently. Emerald continued to pleasure herself thus, her strong legs squeezing Peggy's ribs.

"Ah, Peggy, my dearest," said Emerald in short gasps. "I am riding you like a horse..." The crop met the flesh of Peggy's ass again causing Peggy to toss, which in turn increased Emerald's pleasure. "...do you like this my love? Buck again and again." Emerald's grip tightened on Peggy's hair, causing the girl to jerk and groan. Emerald was thrashing wildly about on her maid's back; her cunt so lubricated that Peggy was fairly drenched with the juices of her mistress. Emerald arched her back; her legs tightened their grip. Her body was rigid and quivering, her hips thrusting violently. She screamed as her orgasm filled her body entirely. She continued to thrust, feeling each wave and its crest, until she fell exhausted from her position as rider.

Peggy's backside was pleasantly crimson, and the girl was positively panting with exertion and excitement. She fell to the lush carpet and into the arms of her mistress, and there they slept until it was time for dinner.

"How I shall miss my pretty little maid," said Emerald dolefully as she rose finally to dress for dinner.

"And I, my lovely mistress," replied Peggy, sadness in her voice.

"I promise to come to Dublin and see you within the next few weeks, darling girl. I can't imagine life without the taste of your sweet cunny on my lips." This comforted Peggy considerably. The girls kissed and finished dressing.

Peggy donned her maid's outfit, and Emerald her elegant evening dress, and the two girls went down to dinner. Peggy followed Emerald as is customary for servants in such households. Peggy could not resist a quick pinch as she walked respectfully behind Emerald. Emerald turned and gave her a sly wink.

# -6-

"I understand, Brigeen, that you distinguished yourself on the occasion of the visit you and Bernadette to paid to Phelim's manor," exclaimed Ursula as she tapped her birch cane on the stone floor.

Brigeen, embarrassed at hearing herself praised so effusively, blushed and stammered that she had endeavored to be a credit to her teachers.

"Yes, glowing reports of your efforts have reached me from several of our devotees, along with praise from the Mercurial Herald himself. Phelim spoke very highly of you when I spoke to him." She paused and gazed at Brigeen. Perhaps it was a jealous stare, perhaps simply a thoughtful one. Finally she continued.

"You have yet to be pierced, of course," she said carefully, and smiled on seeing Brigeen shudder. "Nor have you participated in the initiation of a new girl to the Old Ways." She stood up and pressed the curved end of the cane under the young girl's chin, gently tilting Brigeen's head backwards.

"I wonder whether you would like the newest sweet

thing I seduced this morning at the very same pub where I found you. I think I shall have her watch as you are pierced for your ring." There was, noted Brigeen, an edge of steel in her voice. The cane lifted Brigeen's head still higher. Painfully higher.

"Well, Brigeen? I am waiting for an answer."

"I have taken the vow of obedience, Ursula," stammered Brigeen. "I am yours to command." The cane was cast aside and Brigeen lowered her head in time to see the approving smile on the older woman's sculpted features.

"Good. It is pleasing that your successes and the prospect of presenting yourself on the Isle of Man have not gone to your head," continued the priestess in softer tones. "The new girl is known by the name of Peggy."

Brigeen suddenly remembered with clarity the first weeks of trial in the house of Ursula.

"You are a tenderhearted young thing," Brigeen heard Ursula saying, breaking her reverie. "Obedience is no affectation in our ways, as you well know. The responsibility for introducing Peggy to our ways will be shared between Bernadette and yourself." Brigeen's heart soared with joy at the prospect.

"Peggy had been a combination of lady's housemaid and maid to a Protestant family in Caven, until now," continued Ursula. "So you need not tease her on account of her origins. Still, 'treat each according to her desserts, and who should escape whipping?'" The older woman permitted herself the ghost of a smile before dismissing Brigeen courteously.

On her way upstairs to take her news to Bernadette, Brigeen felt thoroughly excited at the prospect of what awaited her that very week. The thought of being pierced for the ring all the devotees wore depressed her spirits somewhat, but she was aware that she had passed every test put before her so far.

She reached the door of the room she shared with Bernadette and rapped lightly on the door, announcing herself at the same time before entering. Her friend sprawled on the double bed they now shared, painting her toenails with deliberate care.

"Well, Brigeen, I imagine you have the notion to tell me about our tryst with young Peggy from Cavan?" Brigeen felt not a little deflated on realizing that Bernadette had heard the news before she had. Her face fell at the moment Bernadette looked up.

"Witless gosling," Bernadette chided her, amused. "Do you imagine that I am without my spies here? Listen, there is no better news than your piercing or Peggy's initiation. Do you know the old priest at the Church of the Sacred Heart?"

Surprised by what seemed to be an inexplicable digression on Bernadette's part, Brigeen acknowledged that she had exchanged demure salutations with the man from time to time.

"He has a nephew, a beautiful young man soon to be ordained visiting him. Wait until I tell you, Brigeen. The old one is away tonight, officiating at some function or other. The nephew will be at the presbytery alone, my dear. I must have him. I've planned to seduce him and send him over to Phelim's so that he will be sent to the Isle of Man. I know he will be accepted, so pleasing a young thing he is. We have exchanged glances and I know he's ready for the secrets of the Old Way."

Brigeen's heart leapt. This was becoming more exciting with every passing second, she thought.

"Young Joe is almost certainly a virgin, Brigeen. Tell me now, how would you enjoy helping me to cast a spell on the unsuspecting young buck?"

"More than delighted, Bernadette. What an exciting prospect. But how do you know he will receive us?" Brigeen asked, her eyes dancing.

"I spoke to him today in the garden. It's all arranged."

"Does Ursula know about this?" demanded Brigeen suspiciously.

"Indeed she does," replied Bernadette. "She even gave me quite a potent aphrodisiac. She counts it as a reward for having done so well with Phelim." She looked up and grinned roguishly. "Speaking of Phelim, he left a package for you. It contains a bottle of some description from the pleasing noise it makes when shaken."

Brigeen's heart skipped a beat at the mention of the man who had so captured her young girl's fancy. She tore open the box which did indeed contain a special brew of Phelim's own concoction.

Bernadette laughed aloud and said, "It seems that Phelim would like to cast a spell on you himself. He's even gone so far himself to send over his special love brew!

The girls promptly opened the bottle and took several sips, letting the potent liquor work through their systems, making them both feel pleasantly warm.

After some time Brigeen regarded Bernadette quizzically, her head cocked to one side.

"We are to assume that this young Joe knows nothing of our ways, I suppose?"

"He may have heard rumors, but no more than that. Our ways are tolerated and even applauded and upheld by most of the community. Most fear us, and think of our practice as necessary to maintaining the traditional beliefs. Besides, Ursula has the gift of second sight, and she seems to think that young Joe is destined for great things. She encouraged me to spare none of my charms this evening. Ursula feels that a taste of the best we can offer will make a promising fellow feel very kindly toward our ways." She smirked and raised her glass in a toast, giggling.

"Begob, this magical drink is taking its effect on me," Bernadette said, eyeing Brigeen boldly. "Are you feeling at all adventurous, my pretty one?"

"Aye, this whisky is enervating my entire body. What notion has come upon you may I ask, you tireless vixen?"

Bernadette's eyes twinkled with excitement before responding to her question. "Are you willing to put yourself in my hands and trust me, Brigeen?"

With a merry laugh, Brigeen agreed that she was and, at Bernadette's insistence, undressed with haste. She lay down upon the broad bed, her brown eyes wide with interest and anticipation.

"Now, my pretty innocent," Bernadette whispered, "stretch your arms right up. Above your head. Yes, that's right."

Brigeen trembled with sudden apprehension as Bernadette deftly pinioned her wrists with a long silken scarf and secured them to the ornate brass at the head of the bed.

"Bernadette," she whimpered, suddenly fearful, "what are you going to do?"

In answer, Bernadette merely giggled and wormed her slim hands between Brigeen's warm thighs until her fingertips caressed the girl's inner warmth, already ripe with anticipation.

"Surrender yourself wholly to me," Bernadette whispered before nimbly sprawling between Brigeen's outstretched legs. She began flicking her agile tongue to that glowing soft jewel she had come to know so well. Helpless, Brigeen writhed and moaned, arching her hips and thrusting her pelvis hard against Bernadette's soft mouth.

With a sharp cry, as though in unendurable pain, she arched her entire body, her arms straining against the resistance of the bonds around her wrists. She lifted her buttocks and hips all the way off the bed to meet the continuous lapping of Bernadette's insistent tongue. The younger girl sucked and nibbled furiously, undistracted by the violent movements of Brigeen's pleasure.

"Oh, please....no more Bernadette," she cried out. "You will drive me mad!" Her body shuddered with wave after wave of successive pleasure.

Deaf to her entreaties, Bernadette began to work her way up Brigeen's belly, finally stopping at her tits. She began to lick each hardening, erect nipple in turn. She continued to nibble hungrily on the older girl's soft breast and toy with the copse of soft curling hair at the crux of Brigeen's flawless body. Then she descended again and positioned herself between Brigeen's thighs. She applied her artful tongue with dextrous passion, her outstretched fingers now toying with Brigeen's nipples. Brigeen's body jerked up and down, and mewing with pleasure, she received the tireless sucking of Bernadette's mouth. Just as Brigeen thought she would expire from total pleasure, Bernadette lifted her head, panting from her exertions.

"You are an apt and ready pupil," she whispered. "Shall I make you wait for the desserts of this evening, or bring you to a lovely, racking climax now, my love."

Brigeen moaned and writhed on the bed. Her arms, still bound to the headboard, once again strained for release. Her hips continued to gyrate, and as though that were enough of an answer,

Bernadette plunged her cropped head between the wet thighs of her companion and sucked her until the girl was screaming in utter release.

After Brigeen had recovered from her immense pleasure, Bernadette released her and suggested they bathe before visiting their young prey, Joe, the priest's nephew.

"Do you think this strapping young fellow will need the use of the whip?" Asked Brigeen, glancing at the neatly-arrayed collection of thongs and riding crops as she dried herself in front of a tall mirror.

"I somehow doubt it," Bernadette replied. "I don't believe this one will have the predilection for that particular vice. I believe a simple teasing will win this one over."

They made their way down the stairs and outside to keep their appointment with the priest's nephew. They walked slowly under tall chestnut trees beside the path leading through the grounds of Ursula's garden. A hunting owl hooted close behind the pair and a quartet of hawks performed an elaborate quadrille overhead in the shimmering dusk.

"How do you think we should begin?" demanded Brigeen, feeling no less apprehensive and excited than she had when Bernadette had trussed her wrists to the sturdy brasswork of the bed they shared.

"Leave all that to me," Bernadette responded confidently. "When I need to know the sensual inclinations of an Irishman, I need only to look into my own heart." They walked on in companionable silence for some minutes before Bernadette addressed her companion once more.

"You are so accustomed to the gleaming wood godemiche from the green banks of the Isle, that I need hardly remind you that a decent stiff prick is rather different."

Less than twenty minutes later the pair were sitting side by side on a chesterfield of dark green leather in the drawingroom of the parochial house attached to the Church of the Sacred Heart. As the young man, a priest-to-be, expounded in a precise manner upon the doctrine of papal infallibility, Brigeen was conscious of a sense of mounting disgust and disappointment in her breast. Bernadette sensed her mood and, with an imperious pursing of her lips, indicated that she felt it incumbent upon Brigeen to take the initiative.

With a sudden careless movement, Brigeen contrived to spill her cup of clear China tea in her lap. Their host leaped to the rescue, producing a handkerchief to mop hesitantly at Brigeen's soaked dress. As though by accident, her hand seized his and pressed it firmly to the supple warmth of her body.

"Oh, Mr. Noonan," she squealed excitedly, "not there—a little higher. Look, there is some here, in the folds of my dress." Brigeen lay back in a wanton posture and gazed on the young man's countenance with adoring eyes. She noticed over his shoulder that Bernadette was slipping some white powder into Joe's tea. Then seizing the moment, Bernadette pressed her sleek body against his. His face reddening, the young man stumbled back a little. Bernadette innocently held up his cup of tea.

"More tea, Mr. Noonan?" Visibly shaken, Joe Noonan drank the entire contents of the cup in one long gulp. As he turned to set the empty cup on a table, Brigeen hitched up her skirts so that when he again turned he was met with the sight of her nakedness beneath the skirt.

"Oh, Mr. Noonan! Look at her, she is quite scalded, the poor wee thing," cried Bernadette, leaning over him as he stood dumbstruck. She thrust her

96

pelvis savagely against the man's thigh. Joe was thoroughly mesmerized, and so Bernadette silently guided his hand to Brigeen's cleft and grasped his swelling erection that strained at the fly of his trousers.

"Oh, how big and warm it feels!" gasped Bernadette, her eyes wide with excitement.

"Tease me with it, Joe!" Brigeen wailed.

The potion that Bernadette had secreted in his tea was taking hold of the young man. He did not resist Bernadette's adept fingers as she wordlessly unbuttoned the wool pants and bared his throbbing member. It was long and thin and capped with a thick velvety head. Joe leaned over Brigeen and began to rub the tip of his engorged cock on the inside of her gleaming pussy lips. She moaned with pleasure. Bernadette had kneeled next to Brigeen and was lightly squeezing his balls and stroking the solid shaft of his penis.

"Oh, how lovely it feels, Joe," moaned Brigeen. Bernadette had taken to lightly flicking her tongue first over his cock, then sneaking a few tastes of Brigeen. She soon had them both moaning wordlessly.

"I have to fuck you," grunted the young man, blindly attempting to enter the dripping warm cavity between Brigeen's thighs.

"Oh no you don't, me boy-o," said Bernadette quickly. With that she pushed him off the writhing figure of Brigeen. The two of them landed in a heap on the carpet. "Not yet, darling," said Bernadette as she licked his lips and let his tongue enter her mouth. Joe's hands were groping all over Bernadette's sleek body, and finding the hem of her skirt, pushed underneath immediately to her wet and quivering cleft.

"Ah...you banshees," moaned the young man, "you've come here only to tease me, to drive me mad." His fingers continued to probe the enticing fur of Bernadette's cunt, making her squirm with pleasure.

"Not so, lovely lad," she said straddling him, and allowing his engorged member to slip into the cleft of her rear. "We've been sent to show you a sampling of the pleasures that can only be consummated on the Isle of Man."

Joe's eyes were open and his hips were thrusting in uncontrolled thrusts, his hands tightly squeezing the firm flesh of her ass.

"Isle of Man?" he asked, confused.

"Yes, love. We have selected you to be initiated into the Old Ways. It is a great privilege."

His hands were now groping at the front of her corset, and Bernadette continued to wiggle on top of his aching member.

"I can have you if I agree?" he enquired, his voice deep and husky.

"But of course. Our practice is one worshipping earthly pleasures in all their forms. But you have to promise to go see Phelim O'Hara tomorrow. He is expecting you."

Joe's hands were back to exploring the dripping lips of her pussy, and Bernadette writhed at his touch. Remarkably, she remained composed.

Brigeen watched with wonder, her legs spread wide. Her hands found their way to her own aching sex, and she began to tease herself, thoroughly enjoying the spectacle of Bernadette's convincing seduction.

"Anything, you mad tart, I'll do anything to be able to ram my cock in that pretty little cunny of yours. Anything."

"Wonderful, my lovely boy. But..." she said, springing lightly off his gyrating pelvis, "...we only want virgins."

She regarded Brigeen servicing her own clit, and commenced to sucking her friend, while in turn, Brigeen tickled Bernadette's twitching lips and hard little clit. Joe moaned in agony at the sight of the two beguiling girls pleasuring each other.

"Anything...." he whispered.

The girls' young bodies racked in orgasmic convulsions as Joe looked on convinced that the Old Ways were a pleasing alternative to the horrors of the priesthood.

Before leaving the company of Joe Noonan that night, Bernadette left the address of Phelim, saying that he would be expected tomorrow. She lavished one more wild tongue kiss upon the tormented boy's wet lips, and the two girls happily took their leave.

-7-

Brigeen opened the battered Gladstone bag and quickly emptied it of its contents, arraying them on a chair beside the altar in the candlelit drawing room of Ursula's house. She bit her lip apprehensively as she pensively stroked the point of the curved sailmaker's needle before laying it alongside the Scottish tawse, the riding-crop, and the tiny square of the crumpled silk she knew contained a small ring of soft gold.

"My ring," she murmured, her eyes shining brightly in the light of the candles.

Remembering the champagne bucket filled to the brim with crushed ice surrounding a tall bottle of Dom Perignon, thoroughly chilled by now, she scampered lightly across the soft, carpeted floor and brought it to the altar base. Then she stood standing back, arms folded, to survey the scene before her. On a sudden impulse, she leaned over the altar to satisfy herself that the Little Man, and the carved ebony godemiche, and the tapered ceramic cone of the golule were safely out of sight.

101

With a smile illuminating her proud young face, Brigeen fondly recalled her weeks and months of wearing the golule snugly in her tightest orifice until its insertion and extraction had become second nature to her.

At last Ursula, after widening her lovely little rosebud anus painstakingly, had declared that Brigeen's muscles were now so taut and well-disciplined that the use of the strange instrument was no longer necessary.

There was a murmur of voices beyond the carved doors of the altar room, followed by the long creak of the old hinges as they were swung open.

"Brigeen," demanded a familiar voice, "is everything ready?"

"Indeed it is, Sister Bernadette," responded Brigeen standing motionless beside the altar steps. "I take it the person with you is Peggy?"

"Indeed, Brigeen, here she is. What is more, she will assist in piercing you. She knows her duties well enough, I think. Isn't that so, Peggy?

The young girl beside Bernadette looked up fearfully, her eyes adjusting themselves to the gloom, and whispered that she would do her best to give satisfaction.

Spoken like a true housemaid, thought Brigeen as she stared into the stranger's eyes. Peggy, she had been told, was a naive young thing. Brigeen sighed, remembering how quickly the year had flown since her arrival at Ursula's house. She smiled, feeling a pang of regret for pleasures relished and gone.

"Kneel at the altar, Peggy," Bernadette ordered in a strangely quiet voice. The new girl obeyed and Brigeen moved gracefully to her side before bending and slowly raising the hem of the girl's dress.

"Has she been washed thoroughly, Bernadette?" enquired Brigeen, never taking her eyes from the girl's rounded white buttocks illuminated in the pale candlelight.

"She has, Brigeen. In fact, Peggy rather delighted in the feeling that the enema hose gave her sweet little asshole."

Oblivious to the conversation being carried on between the two girls behind her, Peggy hastily whispered silent prayers.

"Have her do the piercing first, Brigeen," whispered Bernadette, bringing her pretty mouth close to her friend's ear. "Then we can do the rest at our leisure."

Brigeen nodded, resigned to the inevitable. "To whom is your maidenhead consecrated, Peggy?"

"To the Great Mother of the Old Ways, and all those on the Isle of Man."

So far so good, thought Brigeen, as her mind spanned the many months since she had knelt at this same altar and given the same hesitant responses. Without waiting for encouragement, Peggy continued the litany, her soft Cavan accent pleasing in the silence of the altar room.

"My vagina is consecrated and sacred; only those initiated are to know me as a woman. Notwithstanding this, my mouth, my hands, my breasts, and my tightest aperture may be employed to advance and enrich the Way in all matters spiritual and temporal." Her responses concluded, Peggy looked up as though seeking approval.

"You have done well, Peggy," commended Bernadette thoughtfully. "Now, let us see if you can assist me to pierce our sister in the Way cleanly and well." Smiling, she smacked the young girl's buttocks loudly.

103

Peggy, blushing furiously, straightened up and stood motionless as Bernadette busied herself with the task of opening the champagne. The wire was unwound with great care.

"This is, as you will appreciate," she remarked, "a trifle unusual. All the same, an initiate's piercing should not pass without due ceremony. Bring the glasses, Brigeen."

Brigeen skipped away, returning a moment later with a trio of tall, fluted champagne glasses. Bernadette eased the cork out of the neck of the bottle with both thumbs. There was a scarcely audible pop, and the Dom Perignon flowed, foaming into the three glasses Brigeen held so carefully in her motionless hand.

"To the ritual piercing of our sister learned in the arts of the Old Way," said Bernadette solemnly as the three figures sipped their champagne in the flickering candlelight.

On a whim, Bernadette turned and kissed Peggy wildly and unexpectedly on the mouth, then did the same with Brigeen. She grinned broadly at the pair before speaking.

"Sit down on the altar steps, Brigeen. Now, Peggy, do you remember what I told you about the ice?"

Her nervousness visible in her eyes, Brigeen sat on the topmost step. She spread her legs wide and pulled the hem of her skirt to her waist. As instructed, she was naked beneath the soft folds of fabric. Her eyes met Peggy's fascinated stare.

"Get on with it, Peggy," snapped Bernadette, picking up the sailmaker's needle and testing its point with her thumb.

Obediently recalling herself to her duty, Peggy filled a small chalice from the altar with ice and looked up expectantly at Bernadette, awaiting further instructions.

"Take the two larger pieces of ice and press them on the folds of her labia." Peggy obeyed eagerly, warming to her task.

"Oh! It's cold!" exclaimed Brigeen as the ice was pressed firmly against the fold of soft flesh fringing her vagina.

Bernadette, amused, laughed coarsely. "This will warm you up, my pretty one," she said as she kneeled between the girl's feet, the long curved needle in her hand. It glittered evilly in the dramatic light of the room.

"Please try not to hurt me, Bernadette," Brigeen pleaded, heedless of Peggy's presence.

Bernadette made no reply. Instead she held the tip of the needle in the dull yellow flame of one of the taller candles on the altar and rotated it slowly in her fingers until it became almost too hot to hold.

"Your flaps ought to be chilly enough now, my pretty one," she cried exultantly. "Give her a hard pinch, Peggy. If she squeals or screeches, she needs more time with the ice."

To Brigeen's great relief, Peggy's pinch was hardly noticeable. Somehow or other she found her voice and announced that she was ready. Smiling, Bernadette resumed her earlier position, pushed Peggy's hand away and—before Brigeen could so much as grit her teeth—pressed the curved needle through the fold of soft white flesh with a determined thrust.

"Hold her firmly. Do not let her move, Peggy!" she ordered and stood up to survey the scene before her. It was, she told Brigeen later, a spectacle which would have pleased one of the more depraved painters of the Baroque—a trembling girl seated on the steps of a curious altar, her labia skewered by a curved needle, her thigh bespattered with blood and her angelic countenance curiously serene. Kneeling at her feet an adoring young initiate, her milk-white hand holding the needle securely between thumb and forefinger.

Bernadette joined the pair a moment later bearing the crumpled silk. Unfolding it, she revealed the tiny ring of gold.

"Watch carefully, Peggy. One of us will do this for you when the time comes."

The needle was withdrawn and the ring replaced it effortlessly. Her fingers gentle and controlled in their movements, Bernadette pinched it shut and whistled softly.

"There, Brigeen. The job is done. Tell me, how does it feel?

"A little painful but no more than that," sighed Brigeen. "At last, I feel truly like one of the Initiated."

"In the fullness of time," laughed Bernadette, "you could find yourself wearing many such rings there. A full dozen, perhaps. One for each of the initiates you come to know, and a thin gold chain lacing them together to symbolize the Holy Mother herself."

"What a beautiful thought," sighed Peggy. Delicately prostrating herself at the older girl's feet, she gently lapped the spattered blood and kissed Brigeen's instep.

Flattered, Brigeen grinned and shook her free as one might an overly friendly puppy.

"For that piece of wanton self-abasement, you shall receive a dozen strokes of the riding crop. Shall I use the tawse, or the Malacca cane, Bernadette?"

Peggy shuddered and drew in her breath sharply.

"A little of each, I think," laughed Bernadette.

She bared Peggy's white buttocks and handed the riding-crop to Brigeen with a merry chuckle.

"Six soft strokes to add a little color to these pretty cheeks," she cried. "Peggy, begin reciting the sacred chant."

Remembering how Loretta had wielded the cane mercifully and gently, Brigeen brought the stiff rod down upon the naked rear of the girl as she whimpered and breathed the holy words. When she was finished, she turned to Bernadette, her face flushed.

"Yes, you have colored her quite prettily, Brigeen," observed Bernadette with a toss of her head. "It's made me positively hot with excitement watching you." She gave Brigeen a lascivious tongue kiss. Then she placed her forefinger in Brigeen's mouth, withdrew it after a few moments, and thoughtfully prodded the warm cleft between Peggy's striped buttocks.

Peggy moaned softy, wiggling her ass a little at the touch of Bernadette's moist finger.

"A lick or two of the tawse now," said Bernadette, rising and reaching for the leather instrument of correction with her free hand. The other continued to tease the younger girl's quivering asshole.

A tailored strap with a tapered tip, it rested lightly in her soft hands. Bernadette stared at it recalling a day long past, then she stepped back.

"Watch this, Brigeen. The secret of using the tawse is to let only the tip make contact with a girl's flesh. A round dozen should suffice for this delicious young angel."

"But the tip will bite like an adder, Bernadette!" protested Brigeen, too late. The tawse swung in a blurring arc and the tip bit into the softness of Peggy's posteriors, eliciting a howl.

"There, that wasn't too much, was it?" Bernadette

enquired solicitously. "Be brave, only eleven more to go!"

Brigeen counted the strokes one by one, biting her lip as she watched Peggy shudder and squirm in what she imagined to be unendurable agony.

The last blow completed, Bernadette dropped the tawse and stamped her small foot in triumph, her face flushed with excitement.

"Begod, Peggy is a brave one. You may comfort her now, Brigeen."

No sooner had she heard the words than Brigeen was on her knees, an arm around the young girl's heaving shoulders. Despite her tears, Peggy retained an icy composure and aloof dignity.

"Is the worst over?" she sobbed in Brigeen's ear, her cheeks wet with tears.

"Not quite," Brigeen murmured, running her pale hands over the girl's bruised haunches, and kissing her wet cheeks. "You have a few more strokes of the Malacca cane to come before you taste the Little Man in your pretty bottom."

Peggy sighed and crouched lower, her elbows on the second step, as Bernadette handed Brigeen the Malacca cane wordlessly. Her lips pursed, Brigeen used the cane with great care, taking pains to avoid those parts of the young girl's buttocks already scored by the crop and the tawse.

All the while, as the cane snapped across the girl's reddened ass, Bernadette danced about the room making lascivious gestures with her hips, her black satin dress swirling around her. She was crying out that the spectacle was making the little lips between her thighs quiver with excitement. She truly looked like a weird sensual banshee.

"Please...No more! No more!" wailed Peggy after the eighth stroke.

"Be thankful you don't have to take the godemiche all the way up your arse on the first day, as I had to!" sneered Bernadette, taking another sip of her champagne.

Mindful of her duties, Brigeen inflicted the remaining strokes briskly, then spun on her heel to fetch the Little Man from the altar, along with the chalice of consecrated oil. She dipped a finger into the thick scented oil and knelt.

"Smear it all the way inside with your finger, just as you would want done to yourself," commanded Bernadette, sipping the last of the champagne from the neck of the bottle. Bernadette watched as Brigeen faithfully obeyed her instructions.

Brigeen noticed that the girl was quite moist in her sweet little furred cleft. Despite her moaning, Peggy was obviously feeling pleasure. Bernadette knelt to join the young initiate kneeling at the altar.

"You tease her clit, Brigeen. The poor bruised girleen could use some comfort, I think."

Bernadette enthusiastically massaged the oil into the shaft of the small object nestling in her palm. She eased Peggy's buttocks asunder, exposing the cleft with its faintly ginger hue and the puckered rosette of her anus. Simultaneously, Brigeen energetically teased the already moist nub of the girl's clitoris. It was just as Brigeen remembered from her own ordeal at the foot of this very altar; her unseen caresses caused Peggy's fleshy rose to quiver in sympathy with the sensations Brigeen's skilled fingers were imparting.

"Oooooh..." moaned Peggy, "that feels so good!" Her whole body quivered in response to the twiddling touch of Brigeen.

"One is gratified to hear that," Bernadette murmured as she pressed the tip of the rigid shaft stealthily against the young girl's anus. She pressed a little harder, grinning.

"Just relax yourself," urged Brigeen, continuing to flick her deft fingers around the dripping cunt of the girl. "It hardly hurts at all, you'll see!"

Peggy threw back her head and uttered a tiny shriek as, little by little, the polished shaft followed the rounded knob into her tight and most secret orifice.

"Dear God!" she moaned. "It's in me. All the way in. Oooooooh!"

"Let yourself relax, my pretty," murmured Bernadette. "Surrender to the pleasure of it."

Her tireless fingers withdrew the shaft and smoothly drove it in deeper a second time.

"Ah, yes. Yes, yes, yes," gasped Peggy, her head on Brigeen's shoulder, while Brigeen's caresses continued more quickly now. Peggy's body writhed over the excitation of her two openings. She moaned and circled her hips in answer to the Little Man and Brigeen's experienced fingers.

An air of raffish celebration enfolded the three of them, Brigeen felt. The pace of Bernadette's thrusts increased until her hand was almost a blur. She was making little animal grunts that melded with the sound of Peggy's pleasure moans. Brigeen could hear her own throat rumbling with lust at the spectacle thus presented.

"Can you feel the pleasure," she said huskily to Peggy, "the unfamiliar delight overcoming you, sharper than any serpent's tooth?"

In reply, Peggy—almost on the brink of hysteria—bucked her body to meet the thrusts of both hands. She threw back her head and howled with a sensual abandon she had never felt before. Taken with the heat of the moment, Brigeen threw her arms around the trembling young girl, grappling with her and kissing her tear-streaked face avidly.

"And now, Peggy, the moment has come for that innocent little sphincter of yours to make the acquaintance of the triumph of the potter's art," observed Bernadette, rising slowly to her feet. She reached for the golule amidst the many other ritual objects.

Peggy did not see the conical object that Bernadette was now bearing. She was too busy being consoled by Brigeen, who was wetly kissing her and toying with her lovely pink nipples that stood erect under her frenzied caresses. Bernadette stood silently admiring the sight of the two nymph-like figures caressing and fondling one another's lithe bodies in the golden glow of the candlelight.

When Peggy seemed ready, Bernadette tilted up her bright red buttocks to receive the pointed tip of the golule. Her tight orifice was already well-greased from the oil of the Little Man and her own juices. The ceaseless groping of Brigeen's fingers also supplied the necessary lubrication. The curious object slid in almost effortlessly, made easier by Peggy's eager thrusts backward, wiggling gleefully on the shaft.

"I simply can't believe this is happening to me," Peggy managed to say. "I had no idea when I met Ursula at the pub that so much pleasure was in store for me."

"Oh, you silly girl," chided Bernadette, "you must have had an inkling of what Ursula was up to."

Peggy smiled slyly and replied, "Well maybe a slight premonition." The three girls broke into warm laughter together. They were all lounging on the plush carpet of the altar room, now sipping glasses of wine. All of them had a pleasant flush on their young cheeks.

111

Peggy at last said, "How can I thank you both?" her moist eyes downcast. "You know, I feel as though I've come into my hour at last."

"There," laughed Brigeen, helping Peggy to her feet, eyeing her anxiously as she essayed her first tentative steps with the waxed ceramic cone snugly resting in her tightest portal. "You are as strong as any Cavan heifer, are you not?" There was a lilt in her youthful voice as she said this. She turned away, busying herself with filling the Gladstone bag with the impedimenta the ritual had required and carrying the ice bucket to the altar room door. Her wide eyes met Bernadette's smoldering glance and she smiled affectionately at the slender young girl standing beside the still younger initiate. A pretty sight they were, too, in the room's soft light.

"To be pierced and also conduct the ceremony in a single evening was rather like adding icing to the cake, Bernadette. Will I be able to cope with my pleasures still to come, do you think?"

"The Horns of Venus, the Lingua Diaboli, Brigeen?" laughed Bernadette gaily. "Ho, yes, you will. After all, Philomena insisted on instructing me in its use the very evening I was pierced, you remember."

Peggy wonderingly followed the pair up the staircase to the room she was to share with them both for many weeks to come. The long white room, made fragrant by the crumbling incense smoldering in a green Tibetan urn, welcomed her joyously.

The open window disclosed a light rain falling over the Garagrove and the island-studded bay. Bernadette bounded across the floor and shut it against the evening chill. A charcoal drawing of Petesouchos, crocodile goddess of the Nile, adorned the wall above the flickering offering candles.

"And is there still honey for the tea?" murmured Bernadette before disappearing as unaccountably as the white rabbit.

Peggy sat down carefully on the bed, finding such a posture as uncomfortable as she had anticipated. This permitted Brigeen to unlace her boots and push her gently backwards so that she reclined on her hip and elbow.

Peggy stared around her; a long walking stick she recognized as a bull's prick was propped against a chest of drawers. Above it hung a meticulously finished sampler which proclaimed, 'Humility is the last trap awaiting seekers in the search of truth.' What had she come to? she wondered dreamily in the incense-laden air. A minute later she found herself sipping strong tea laced with whiskey.

Brigeen suddenly went to the chest of drawers and yanked opening the lowest drawer. Barely containing her mirth, she produced an object which made Peggy sit bolt upright. Describing it many years later, Peggy recalled with vivid clarity its shape and hue despite her initial incredulity at beholding it.

A pair of female faces not more than two inches in height and joined at the back, displayed sharp noses. To Peggy's stupefaction, from the mouths of both goddesses a tongue over seven inches in length curved upwards.

"The Horns of Venus," explained Brigeen, her flawless face wreathed in smiles.

"What can it be for? Who made it?" gasped Peggy, turning the object over and over in her hands.

"Wait and see, you pretty innocent," tittered Bernadette, tenderly kissing the tips of both tongues before laying the object aside. "It was made on the Isle of Man for worship purposes. Soon Brigeen and I will be called to the Isle to perform our ritual defloration. Unfortunately, this beautiful object is meant for total penetration, so we are forbidden that delight as of yet."

Peggy's perplexity increased as Bernadette rose and slowly began to remove her clothing. Pleased to have an audience, Bernadette took her time. When her breasts were bare, she clasped her hands behind her head to display the small apple-smooth mounds to best advantage. She cupped one, and then the other, her eyes never straying from Peggy's wide stare. She then slowly unfastened her skirt and let it drop to the floor, revealing the fact that she was entirely naked under her skirts.

Brigeen, feeling left out, came up behind Bernadette and squeezed her little nipples. Bernadette leaned back moaning softly. Brigeen, also excited to have an audience, undressed slowly with the help of the already-naked Bernadette. The two fell on the bed, their young bodies quivering with anticipation. Hands were groping heatedly at one another's breasts, mouths met in wet kisses, tongues lashed at moist lips. Peggy watched in utter fascination.

Brigeen reached across the writhing body of Bernadette for a tiny phial of oil on the bedside table. She poured a bit into her palm and proceeded to rub the thick drops onto the two curving tongues of the Horned Venus. Her slender fingers massaged the oil into the dark tropical wood, carefully oiling the pointed tips while she grinned wickedly at Bernadette. She at last turned her deft hands to the already wet cunt of her young companion. She slowly massaged the pink lips of Bernadette's labia, giving the little gold ring there a knowing, gentle tug.

Bernadette moaned and began to tickle her own

114

clit, as Brigeen did the same to herself using the remaining oil to lubricate her plump red pussy lips.

Bernadette stood and grasped the Horned Venus. Then looking over at Peggy, who sat in rapt attention, she said, "Watch this well, Peggy dear."

"Remember, Bernadette, do not impale yourself entirely on the pretty toy in your excitement," said Brigeen languidly.

With that Peggy stared at the pair who held the wooden faces between them. The outstretched wooden tongues flicked the pulsing clits of both girls simultaneously. Bernadette and Brigeen began rocking their hips in matching thrusts. Their free hands toyed with one another's nipples. Their upper bodies met and they touched nipples as they kissed wildly. Their young hips swayed back and forth. The wild wooden tongue teased and tickled the lips of their oiled pussies. Both were kneeling, face to face on the bed, their bodies covered with sweat as they moaned in pleasure together. Bernadette reached around her young friend's waist, still holding the Horned Venus with her other hand. She began to tickle Brigeen's little hole that was exposed because of her spread knees. This titillation only strengthened Brigeen's gyrations. She returned the touch of Bernadette, seeking the girl's puckered rose from behind. She ran her finger lightly and quickly around the hole, teasing the other girl. Soon both had embedded their probing fingers inside the tight portals of one another.

The wooden tongued object remained between them, giving them both relentless pleasure. Both girls were careful not to thrust so hard in their excitement so as to shove the stiff tongues into their virginal, sopping lips.

With an inarticulate screech of unearthly pleasure, Bernadette arched her back and achieved her

115

climax, her body shuddering and writhing with almost inhuman ferocity. An answering shudder and a succession of low growls from Brigeen's throat a dozen heartbeats later announced her climax, and from the sound of her throaty call, satiation.

Panting and still embracing, they let the Horned Venus fall to the bed. They regarded Peggy languidly as they held each other in trembling arms.

At last Brigeen giggled, "Are we to share the inexperienced attentions of our new friend, my love, or are we to compete for her favors? Let's have her between us like the filling in a meat sandwich," chuckled Bernadette playfully.

The three then enmeshed in a tumble of young flesh, Peggy in the middle, wriggling and writhing with erect nipples and grasping hands. The two girls on the outside of this unlikely union grasped one another's fleshy buttocks as Peggy—gleefully happy to be included in such pleasure—began to grind her hips, her mount crashing against Brigeen's, while her ass served as a soft fleshy cushion of friction for Bernadette's hungry gyrations. The three of them bucked and groped until they were simultaneously wracked with powerful sobs of pleasure. The three looked like flushed goddesses, the Muses entangled in one another's arms.

Peggy soon fell fast asleep from so much exhaustive pleasure.

Brigeen whispered softly to Bernadette, "A promising girl, I think," as she nuzzled her slender companion's ear.

"Mmmmm, yes," replied Bernadette languorously. "If she distinguishes herself in the

116

weeks ahead, perhaps she will accompany us to the Isle for the festival." And with that the two girls drifted into a warm sleep.

-8-

The preparations on the Isle of Man had started. The High Priest was anxious about the selection of the girls to present to the High Priestess. He was flushed by the memory of so many a young nymph who had danced at this same festival year after year. It was his favorite of all the rites and rituals of the Way. The defloration.

The High Priest's cock grew stiff as he recalled the screams of agony and delight as the girls with their selected partners engaged in the process of losing their virginity one by one in the temple. Their thighs, and the cocks of their respective partners were then inspected for the sacred blood. He sighed rubbing his stiff member through the folds of his robes. How he loved the wild orgies that ensued.

It was written that the group of young initiates who performed the most exciting sexual act, an act so inspiring that it proved to incite the rest of the worshippers to a frenzy, would be invited to stay on the Isle as consorts of the High Priestess herself, enjoying power and luxury for their reward. Of course, all the acts were to consist of young boys with boys, and young girls with girls.

"Ahh, yes, this year should prove most passionate," he said to himself.

It was known to the Islanders that the High Priestess had been in a rage for some time now. It seemed that she was becoming harder and harder to please, her sexual appetite ravenous. Well, thought the Lord of the Isle, if they were unable to find a group of young initiates to stay as her consorts.... He didn't even want to think about it. There would surely be some that were exhilarating young virgins. After all, they were arriving from all over Europe for the Festival, and the Priests and Priestesses throughout had been given orders to train the young things well. The Isle only wanted the best for the sacred ritual.

He smiled again at the thought and gave his engorged member one last tug before sighing and rising to oversee the preparations firemakers and wreathmakers.

# -9-

An elegant buffet had been laid out in what was normally the Great Master's dining room. Brigeen stared around her. Everything, she saw, was red, a startling crimson. Red tablecloths were festooned with swags of dark green laurel and, incongruously, shamrocks. Crystal vases of bright red rosebuds stood beside the Matterhorn of food. A brace of chefs in tall white hats carved slices of Limerick ham and paper-thin slivers of darkly sinister prosciutto, a gift from an Italian Mercurial Lord who knew the Great Master well.

She turned to see Bernadette neatly extracting a strawberry from a long silver platter and virtuously avert her eyes from several deep bowls brimming with raspberries and cream. Naturally, there was pink champagne in abundance, a treat for the three finalists.

Blushing, Brigeen thought of all she, Bernadette and Peggy had experienced so far. The spectacle to which Bernadette lightly referred to as our 'refined lesbian show' had met with wild approval and had carried the trio to the final stage of the contest.

The three girls had first performed an engaging game of licking and teasing each other for Phelim and Ursula. The two older believers in the Way thought that they were well trained and ready to attend the Isle Festival. Yet their skills now needed to be approved by the Master himself. He knew better than any on the mainland what the High Priestess's likes and dislikes were. Brigeen was nervous about performing in front of this strange older man, but Bernadette's continuous coaching and easy way put her a little more at ease.

Despite Bernadette's misgivings, Peggy had insisted on telephoning the daughter of the house in Cavan in which she had formerly been of service. Her performance with Emerald in front of the other two girls had left the four of them frolicking in a naked sweaty heap on a broad bed in Ursula's house. To their joy, including Ursula's, the girl had decided to stay on at the house for a little more education. She was a willing learner in the Arts of the Way.

Brigeen started on hearing her name called. She scurried to her inconspicuous seat beside Bernadette and Peggy. They sat on enormous soft cushions on the floor, the air heavy with incense and mysterious candlelight. The girls eyes were shining with expectation for the final judging. A furtive glance around the room took in the vast paunch of the Lord Master of all Europe. He sat at ease on his enormous throne. Brigeen's eyes widened as she noticed the girl-child that he fondled at his right. She apparently was his constant companion, and rumored to have the gift of second sight.

"Isn't she marvellously and unaffectedly sensual?" whispered Peggy in Brigeen's ear. "The long and exquisitely light blonde hair accentuates her slenderness quite delightfully."

The girl at the Lord's feet was Mary. She was wearing a sleeveless garment cut like a tunic, rounded at the neck, tied at the waist with a golden cord and abruptly ending no lower that halfway down her thighs.

"A very expensive transparent tissue, probably gauze of some kind or other," hissed Bernadette admiringly.

As Mary turned to whisper in the Lord Master's ear, Brigeen sat up with astonishment. She could see two brand marks, Celtic mystery symbols, on either shoulder of the young girl.

"Ah...she's been to the Isle, I see," said Bernadette, looking at the marks on the girl's back. "And so young." There was a trace of jealousy in her voice.

Brigeen looked around the opulent room with its huge altar of enormous phalli and vaginal symbols cut from stone. There were garlands and flowers and burning candles to the Great Goddess. She caught the eye of a dark priest sitting in splenid robes. He had the handsomest and cruellest face that she had ever seen. Her gaze was drawn instinctively to his, for he was staring at her with fierce, burning eyes that swept her until she felt stripped naked of her simple white novice's cape. She found herself strangely pleased to be regarded in such a manner by him.

"That priest certainly is using his powers on you," whispered Bernadette, observing the mesmerized stares of the young man and her friend.

The reassuring sound of Bernadette's voice shattered the hypnosis, and Brigeen looked back to the

Lord and the pretty young thing at his side. Through the transparent garment worn by the young girl, Bernadette could clearly see her budding breasts. The object of her scrutiny turned suddenly and smiled, mysteriously aware of Brigeen's eyes on her. Brigeen could see her enchanting mons veneris lightly covered with delicate blonde curls. With a rakish wink, Mary turned again and kissed the Lord Master's bald head. Her rear, noticed Brigeen, was every bit as adorable and enticing as her front, for below her branding marks she displayed a long sinuous back like that of a panther and the bottomcheeks like two exquisitely round apples.

At the Lord Master's nod, a young initiate from Spain got up and curtsied. She went to a corner of the room where a group of young men sat in front of drums and cymbals. The drums began to sound and the beautiful Spanish girl began to sing. It was a strange and almost frightening sound she made. It was the ancient song of the Old Way, and her voice was deep and melodious.

Mary rose, stepping away from the Lord Master's great chair. She went to the center of the room and began to dance. It was a queer and conventional dance at first, her movements slow and languid. Then the rhythm began to speed up. Mary began to make lewd gestures, her diaphanous gown flying about her. She thrust her small hips around in amazing gyrations. She suddenly tore her small dress from her impeccable body. Then she was moving this way and that with the most agility Brigeen had ever seen. She wore nothing but a tiny gold chain that went around her taut belly, and Brigeen was not surprised to note that it was attached to two glittering rings pierced through both of the young girl's labia. She tossed her head and moved in perfect synchronicity with the deep thud of the drums and the Spanish girl's beautiful, weird singing. She tore at her breast almost wildly; she touched her body unashamedly. Mary was totally lost in the music as she knelt on the ground, thrusting her hips and opening the glistening lips of her cunt, wildly displaying her quivering vulva.

It was almost erotically unbearable to watch. Bernadette was motionless on her cushion, watching in total delight the lewd, pagan dance of Mary. Suddenly the drums and song ceased, and Mary fell to the ground on her back, her long legs spread, her perfect breasts heaving, the nipples erect from exertion.

"That was marvellous," sighed Bernadette breathlessly. "She is a goddess to be sure."

Brigeen could only silently nod, so great was her amazement at the spectacle she had just witnessed.

The effect of the dancing girl on the Lord Master was bizarre in the extreme. As the young girl moved about the room, seducing everyone present, he threw back his head. His eyes rolled back so that only the whites could be seen; his body contorted and racked in rhythm with hers.

At last, Mary seemed to regain consciousness. She rose from the ground gracefully and threw her simple tunic over her head, to the rumble of appreciation from the followers. She returned to the Lord Master's side; he promptly began to touch her sweating body everywhere.

All eyes watched in appreciation as he squeezed the erect nipples of the girl roughly. A sharp intake of breath from the watching crowd could be heard as he slipped his hand under the transparent gauze of her dress and visibly slipped his fingers into her dripping pussy. She was obviously pleased to have the admiration of not only the Lord Master, but the

126

entire crowd. She theatrically moved her hips over his groping hand.

The Lord Master grabbed her hand and thrust it over his obviously erect cock. The two engaged in a passionate exchange of caresses until both were crying out with pleasure. It was an incredible spectacle, and all present appreciated it immensely.

When the crowd had regained its composure, the dark priest who had caught Brigeen's eye stood and suggested that they feast before the testing commenced. Because all the food was strangely sensuous in nature, the erotic climate was only heightened during the meal. Couples and groups of initiates all sat together, quietly discussing their roles in the ceremony.

Brigeen glanced around at her surroundings. Many handsome young people sat in white robes amidst an atmosphere of luxury and opulence. The topic on everyone's lips was the coming Festival. Somehow she felt sure that she and her companions would soon be sailing for the mysterious Isle of Man.

After the feasting, the drums sounded again to announce the beginning of the judging. Bernadette, Brigeen and Peggy sat nervously together, anxiously awaiting their turn to perform in front of their peers in the Way.

What proceeded was almost dreamlike. Beautiful young people of all nationalities performed the most exotic, lewd sexual acts. The one stipulation of the contest was that the virginity of all the initiates be maintained. This meant that girls could be had in their tightest portals, or in their mouths. Their clits and lips could be teased, but they could not be penetrated. For the young boys, they could be entered in the ass, and could enter one another, but they were not to take the virginity of any of the young girls, nor be had by any initiates already deflowered.

Naturally, what ensued were some of the most creative contortions and variations on the giving and receiving of pleasure. The atmosphere was tense, because all the young people were anxious to heave themselves on one another and fuck each other in wild abandon. This tension lent itself to the flaming sensuality of the event.

Tall, lean boys from Scandinavia writhed together in a mass of taut muscles, golden bodies and golden hair. They licked and sucked one another so lasciviously that Brigeen felt her thighs dampen at the sight of their wantonness.

Dark young girls from Italy presented a fine display of passion as they wriggled delightfully over one another's faces. Bernadette squeezed Brigeen's hand, never lifting her gaze from the beautiful young initiates' performance.

Soon it was time for the young girls from Ireland to perform. Brigeen flushed with pleasure to see Phelim conspicuously seated amongst other Mercurial Heralds in their dark robes.

Bernadette nodded for the drums to begin, and a low, rhythmic pounding filled the room. Peggy produced the Horns of Venus from beneath her flowing robes and a low rumble of appreciation could be heard. She began to dance a ring around Brigeen and Bernadette. As she moved around them, she slowly undid the ties to their robes. Soon the two older girls stood naked and shaking before one another. Brigeen felt that she had never seen Bernadette before. She was aroused tremendously by the fact that she had an audience. By the look in Bernadette's and Peggy's smoldering eyes they, too, felt the wild heat of the moment.

To the pagan beat of the drums, Brigeen and Bernadette fell into one another's arms. Brigeen knelt slowly, her full hips rotating to the beat, and her mouth began to work Bernadette's tits. First one and then the other. As she bent her legs, she felt Peggy come behind her and tease her asshole with the Horned Venus. Bernadette threw her head back in pleasure at the insistent tongue of Brigeen on her small, firm breast. Peggy, holding the Horned Venus so that one tongue licked at the oiled pucker of Brigeen's prone rosette, began to tease her own clit. Slowly, Brigeen traced her tongue down the flat belly of Bernadette who was grinding her hips slowly in time with the ancient drum pattern. The three young girls made a beautiful picture, all servicing each other.

As the beat of the drums quickened, Brigeen flicked her tongue more viciously inside the lips of Bernadette's gleaming wet cunt. Her head rotated lovingly with each gyration of her friend's hips. Peggy, now naked behind Brigeen, began to drive the wooden tongue of the Horned Venus gradually, but surely into the kneeling girl's ass, simultaneously pumping her hips so that the facing tongue massaged her eager pulsing nether lips. Peggy was now able to lean over Brigeen while still driving the tongue of Venus into Brigeen's rear entrance, and pinch the already erect nipples of Bernadette. By thrusting the pleasure toy deeper and deeper into Brigeen, Peggy was able to meet Bernadette's wet lips, and they engaged in a passionate kiss. Brigeen continued to lap at the cunt of her partner, her tongue probing deeper inside the smooth pink lips as she was pushed forward by the embuggering thrusts of Peggy and the diabolic Horned Venus. The three girls were in perfect synchronization with the rhythm of one another's bodies, and with the sound of the drums. They were all three caught in a maelstrom of abandon. Their juices flowed so freely that the watchers could see the glistening honey on their mouths, their fingers, their swirling cunts. It was breathtaking when all three girls began to shudder and quicken as the waves of climax gripped them.

They all began to moan and shake with orgasmic pleasure. The waves continued on and on, and the three young girls continued pleasuring each other. Peggy thrusting her tongue deep into Brigeen's tight little aperture, as Brigeen sucked and moaned at Bernadette's clit, her tongue probing the fleshy depths. Peggy continued to writhe on the tip of the Horned Venus, which was gleaming wet from her cum. Meanwhile she and Bernadette kissed and teased one another's engorged nipples. Soon they were all screaming ecstasy to the loud beating of the ritual drums. They collapsed on the floor in a heap of arms, legs, and naked flesh, made more beautiful by the sheen of perspiration that covered their young bodies. As Brigeen began to regain her senses after the intensity of orgasm after orgasm, she could hear the approving cries of the crowd.

# -10-

When the girls returned to the house in Dublin, they found Ursula waiting for them by the front gate. She was beaming, her arm draped around Philomena's square shoulders.

"Congratulations, my beauties," she called. "I spoke to Phelim only moments ago, and he said you were all breathtakingly beautiful, and aroused even the Lord Master himself."

When the girls arrived closer, she gave each one a loving kiss and ushered them inside.

"We must have a celebration tonight. You have made me so proud. You are all going to the Isle for the Festival! Philomena, put some Dom Perignon on ice; we are to have a party."

Bernadette, Brigeen, and Peggy were all flushed with excitement as they entered the warmth of Ursula's house. Their capes were taken from them and they fell into the soft couches in the sitting room where a fire was roaring in the hearth.

Philomena reappeared with four bottles of champagne, the first chilling on ice. The girls settled in to tell Ursula about the exciting afternoon. Philomena popped the cork on the champagne, and the three initiates were saluted for their unerring obedience to the rules of the Way.

"Tell us, Ursula, what should we expect on the Isle?" asked Bernadette, already tipsy from the champagne.

"Well," said Ursula, in a serious tone, "much of what happens there is sacred and secret, so I cannot disclose everything. I will prepare you for your parts in the rite, and that is all. The rest you will have to find out when you get there."

"Will we be branded?" asked Brigeen, a little fear showing in her voice. "We saw the Lord Master's consort dance, and she had two marks on her shoulders."

"I cannot say, my darling. That is up to the whim of the High Priestess." She ruffled Brigeen's soft hair affectionately. "Do not fret about that now, my dear. Just feel honored that you are going to lose your sacred virginity on the most magically powerful island in all of Europe."

The women sat in comfortable silence drinking for a while, and then Ursula jumped up suddenly with a devilish grin on her severely beautiful face.

"Peggy, have you the Horn of Venus with you?" she enquired.

Peggy wordlessly held up the curious object, brandishing it with a flourish and saying to the wooden face, "You, my lovely, won the contest for us." She licked the curled tongue suggestively.

"Hand that wicked thing this way," demanded Ursula. "Philomena," she said, turning to the

133

woman, "shall we demonstrate for these virgins the true usage of this sacred object?"

"With pleasure, Sister Ursula," said the older girl, also grinning lasciviously. She walked over to Ursula and promptly pulled back the bodice of Ursula's black satin gown. So taken was she by the idea of performing the Horned Venus Dance with Ursula, she immediately began to bite and suck the older woman's large, rounded breasts. Ursula squealed girlishly and also tore at Philomena's satin bodice, so that they stood, two regal priestesses, with their breasts bared for one another's pleasure.

The three younger girls sat in a close cluster on the velvet divan, all eyes shining with delight at the rare opportunity of seeing someone else perform for them.

"Begod," exclaimed Bernadette thickly, "I do believe they are to frig one another with the blasted thing. This should be exceptional." And then she plunged her hand under Brigeen's white robe, probing for her mons veneris. Upon finding the treasure, she tugged and teased the girl's moist little hairs. Brigeen gasped playfully and reached her arm around Peggy's shoulder to find a ripe nipple ready to the touch. All the girls kept their eyes on the two women standing before them pleasuring each other.

Philomena had suckled Ursula's breasts until the nipples were engorged and pointed with excitation. Ursula growled and reached down, taking Philomena's nipples between her thumb and forefinger. She teased and stroked until Philomena's nipples were also painfully erect.

Ursula pushed Philomena away and hastily tore at the remaining garments worn by the the younger woman. Her hands tore the fabric clear away, revealing the long, sleek body of Philomena glow-

134

ing in the firelight. Ursula fell to her knees and flicked her tongue out teasing the hair that was a perfect dark copse of curls, shining wet already. Philomena moaned and pressed her hips forward to meet Ursula's mouth, but Ursula teased her more, withdrawing her tongue as Philomena pushed forward.

The girls continued to stare, their gaze riveted on Ursula and Philomena, yet they managed to slide more closely together to titillate one another during this erotic show.

Philomena had—in frustration at being teased—bent down to rip the remaining fabric of Ursula's dress away. Now they both knelt naked before one another, their tongues darting wildly in and out of one another's lips, their hands teasing each other's clit. Both wore many rings along the furred fringe of their labia.

"How lovely they look," murmured Brigeen, slightly pumping her pelvis against the probing fingers of her friend.

Ursula tugged on the tiny gold rings that looped through Philomena's labia, and Philomena moaned more loudly. They were so close now that their breast tips grazed each other, and they slowly swayed in response to the enormous pleasure of each other's hands.

"My girl," said Ursula, "you are as slippery as an eel. I do think you're ready for the pleasures of the Venus."

Philomena simply moaned in response, her hips moving in small circles over Ursula's hand. With her free hand, Ursula reached for the Horned Venus. She gracefully inserted one of the curving tongues all the way inside herself, her plump, dripping lips closing around the unyielding wood. She groaned

135

deeply with pleasure. She then lay back against some cushions resting on the plush carpet.

"Come to me, my love," Ursula beckoned Philomena. The other tongue of the device jutted from Ursula's pussy.

Philomena, without hesitation flung herself heartily on the curving phallic tongue. The two women's bodies met, Philomena's large breasts gracefully falling to meet Ursula's. She had thrust herself so violently on the object that the double-sided face was lost between her body and Ursula's. Their pelvic bones touched, and both made to slow pumping movements. Their lips met in hot kisses, their nipples pressed to one another.

The three younger girls all watched in utter fascination. They were so moved by the scene of the two rocking so sensuously, Philomena atop Ursula, impaled by the wooden tongues, that they had rearranged their now-totally-naked bodies on the divan so that they could explore and pleasure one another while enjoying the fantastic scene.

"That's it girl!" called out Ursula. "That's it, fuck me, fuck me harder!"

Philomena took no pause, and sped up her thrusts over Ursula while driving the other tongue inside herself more deeply. Ursula began to moan softly, soon joined by Philomena.

Philomena raised herself upright and began to move her hips in a way that the girls had never seen. It was beautiful to watch. Her flat belly wriggled like a writhing snake, causing her hips to buck against Ursula's writhing body beneath her. Philomena moved like a woman possessed, her arms raised over her head, her body given over to total abandon.

Ursula arched her back and received the movements. The two women were now cooing and growling. Philomena began to gasp, her hips moving wildly. The girls could see that the glistening juices flowed freely on Philomena's spread thighs.

The two women impaled on the Horned Venus began to scream together, Ursula thrusting her hips up harder and harder, as Philomena drove hers down. They continued in simultaneous orgasm for minutes, as wave after as wave of convulsions ran through their bodies.

After they had fallen into each other's arms, and removed the soaking tongues from their still fluttering pussies, they looked up astonished to see the young initiates in a tumble of groping hands and pink lips against pinker flesh of wet virgin pussy. It was a lovely thing to behold the young girls abandoning themselves to such pleasure, moved to such an extreme by the fucking of Ursula and Philomena.

Brigeen had placed her pretty head in the lap of Peggy, who was in turn hungrily sucked by Bernadette. Brigeen had straddled her long legs over Bernadette's and she was grinding her wet cunt lips into the convenient knee of her friend. Soon they, too, were groaning and crying out in satisfaction. Their young bodies shuddered with orgasmic electricity.

The women regarded each other appreciatively in the warmly glowing room. They were on the fourth bottle of champagne, and all of them had a light in their eyes from having been freshly fucked or caressed.

"Well, my young initiates," said Ursula after a long silence, "I think that you will quite enjoy the excitement on the Isle. I believe I have trained you well."

"If we get frigged like the two of you, I won't have any complaints," Bernadette said, smiling drunkenly.

"You won't have to worry about that, darling," said Philomena wickedly. "You'll be fucked until you're screaming for mercy in the name of the Great Queen herself"

The three girls looked at one another and burst into hysterical giggles.

"Don't laugh too soon," said Ursula, cryptically. "Now it's time for a bath. Off you go, my young ones. Philomena and I will join you presently. Perhaps we shall all sleep in my bed tonight."

The girls scampered off to bathe, excited about the prospect of a night in Ursula's huge bed, and the pleasure they might enjoy while in it.

*-11-*

There were a few days of preparation before the girls at last set sail for the mysterious Isle of Man. There were tearful farewells from Emerald, Philomena and Ursula on the dock at Dun Laoghair. Ursula's last words were for them to be brave. It seemed like such a foreboding good-bye to the girls who were so excited to leave.

The fog was low on the Irish Sea. The small boat taking the girls was chartered by Phelim O'Hara. On board were his boys, initiates who also had been selected to attend the festival.

Brigeen's heart skipped when she saw that Phelim was to be at the festival. She felt a flutter between her sensitive legs as she once again was overpowered by his kingly demeanor. His full head of white hair danced in the wind, his blue eyes sparkled cruelly when they met Brigeen's adoring stare.

"Ah...my pretty Donegal maid is come. I am so

pleased." He stroked her head, and she felt shudders of delight run down her spine.

Bernadette had already settled in next to Joe, the young man she and Brigeen had introduced into the Way. Bernadette was flushing prettily as she gaily chatted with the young man. Brigeen marked that he looked different than last she saw him. He was cool and composed, his sexuality oozing from him like strong perfume. He was a perfect initiate. As always, Ursula had been right. He did look promising, wrapped in his cape.

Peggy had cast her eyes around the boat, but found no one there that struck her fancy. She was a bit downcast at leaving Emerald behind. She sat close to Brigeen, nervously holding her hand.

The trip was not long, and soon the rocky coast of the Isle could be seen. There was a nervous tension amongst all the initiates on board. They knew nothing, or at best, very little of the secret rites of the Isle. The small schooner pulled into a private dock.

"There doesn't seem to be anyone here," whispered Bernadette in Brigeen's ear. "I hope they don't just push off, leaving us poor virgins here to fend for ourselves." She was laughing, but there was an edge of fear in her voice that Brigeen had never heard before.

"Don't worry, love," the older girl said, rumpling Bernadette's chestnut hair. "We'll have a grand time." Brigeen had tried to sound convincing, but she knew there was a note of apprehension in her voice.

The Isle looked terribly ominous. Bernadette was right; there was no sign of life anywhere. Phelim began to herd the young initiates to the gangplank. Brigeen found the sound of his rich voice reassuring.

They were led off the dock and to the mouth of a

cave just beyond the beach. Its wide mouth emitted no light, and it had the look of a yawning dragon.

"Hell-mouth," muttered Bernadette, clutching Peggy's hand. "We're walking into hell."

"Silence, girl!" barked Phelim. The three girls jumped. They had never heard so serious a tone from the Mercurial Herald. "You are entering sacred ground. You will not speak unless told to. You have no rights on this consecrated ground until your bodies, and souls, are anointed by the High Priestess." Phelim's tone was so deep and ferocious, Peggy let out a little yelp of fear. "Silence! Or I shall have to reprimand you severely."

Although his sharp speech frightened Brigeen immeasurably, she also felt a strange thrill at the cruel note in it.

They walked into the pitch dark opening of the cavern without another sound. As they walked in utter darkness for some time the girls clutched at one another, stumbling sometimes over their own feet. They were so afraid they failed to notice that the surface they were walking upon was worn smooth. It seemed an eternity that they were led, and then gradually a light could be seen. This tiny glow became larger and larger as they stumbled along blindly. Soon the cavernous tunnel was lit by a strong orange radiance.

They were roughly pushed into the light. All the initiates blinked, attempting to adjust their eyes to the blazing torches of the huge underground chamber. When their eyes did adjust a ripple of awe and a collective gasp came from the small group.

They were standing at the bottom of a huge underground theater. The rock walls rose high; the torchlight leaped off the crags and angles of the amazing vault. There were cuts into the center wall

142

forming stone balconies high above the arena floor. The floor was smoothly polished granite that gleamed in the firelight. Bernadette turned to Brigeen, her eyebrows raised, her eyes filled with not a little fear. Brigeen squeezed her hand to calm her so that she would not cry out or speak.

Suddenly there was the sound of drums. It echoed throughout the chamber. Upon the high dais, a man appeared. He was accompanied by several young men and women all held by collars connected to a leash. The man was garbed in a flowing purple robe which, when he approached the edged of the balcony, flowed over the side like strange purple liquid.

The drums ceased as the naked initiates on the chains arranged themselves at the man's feet.

"I am the High Priest." His voice thundered through the great hall. "Welcome followers. Welcome Phelim, Mercurial Lord, magician, and favorite of the High Priestess, our Mother, our Goddess."

The mere mention of her sent anguished ripples through the small group of initiates standing beneath the High Priest.

He was an older man who carried his body proudly. Beneath his purple robe he wore a classic white gown tied with an intricate Celtic belt. He had long, flowing white hair and black almond eyes.

"Phelim," he thundered, "I shall start the ritual inspection of the initiates immediately."

"Yes, Lord," Phelim replied humbly.

The fact that Phelim was subservient to this man made Brigeen, Bernadette, and Peggy more afraid.

"I shall send my nymphs of Ireland up first, my lord," shouted Phelim.

With a shove, the girls were directed to an opening in the chamber wall.

There was a steep staircase lit by smaller torches.

The girls took their time walking up the stairs, taking the moment to whisper reassurances to one another.

Upon arriving at the top of the steep winding stairwell, they entered another room, very large, but not so large as the theater from whence they came. This room had lower ceilings, and there were cushions and heavy rugs covering the stone floor. There were cryptic drawings on the walls, images of the sacred moon, and renderings of the Great Queen in all her manifestations.

The girls stood in the center of the room, in silent expectation. From a hidden door the High Priest whirled in, his robes flowing around him, his initiates following obediently. When their chains were dropped by the High Priest, they walked to the far corner of the room and arranged themselves in languid poses. They looked quite beautiful to Brigeen, their young bodies oiled, the total nakedness made more obvious by the thick golden collars around their necks. She felt a little envious and tore her eyes away.

"Beautiful young initiates," said the High Priest with a gentleness in his tone that made the three young girls relax, "welcome to the the Isle of Man, and the Festival of Venus." He walked to each of the girls and placed a fatherly kiss on each forehead. "I presume that you have been trained well by our illustrious sister, Ursula?"

The girls nodded silently.

"Good. I must lay consecrated hands on you. I am going to check your sacred rings." And without so much as a pause, he thrust his hand between Peggy's thighs past the opening in her robes. "Ah, very moist, I see. Good, good girl." He then savagely tore open the fabric of her soft robe and fondled her breasts roughly. Peggy let out a squeal

144

and was immediately spanked on her white backside.

"That is what you get for your presumption. You must not speak until you are anointed." And then he slapped her full young breasts, not too hard, but enough to redden the strawberry nipples into an erect state. Peggy stood quivering and naked to the High Priest's inspection. He parted her legs with his soft leather boot, and then in agile fashion, dropped to his knees and thrust his tongue violently into the furred cleft there. He let his tongue tease the girl, and finding her perfectly pierced, let the tip of his tongue tug on the tiny golden ring a little. Peggy, now thrusting her hips a tiny bit forward to meet his tongue, was immediately reprimanded with a smart slap to her pussy. She almost cried out, but bit her lip instead, nearly drawing blood.

The High Priest then led Peggy to a pile of soft cushions, and laying her on her back, ordered her to spread her legs. Obediently, Peggy complied. The High Priest opened the fleshy lips of her labia, made shiny by his saliva, and proceeded to examine the authenticity of her virginity. Peggy tried to relax and not struggle against the discomfort, or the pleasure, but her young hips began to twitch a little despite her attempts at self-control.

"You shall be punished for that," said the High Priest, not looking up from his task.

When he was done between her legs, he roughly turned her over on the pillows and gave her another sound smack on her already marked ass. His hand came down again, and then again. Peggy dutifully remained silent. He then stuck his long forefinger into his mouth and, drawing it out again well lubricated, he quickly jammed it into Peggy's tiny asshole.

"Very, very nice," crooned the Priest. "Well muscled, tight reflex, and a seasoned portal." He allowed himself a little luxury and diddled his finger about a bit longer than was necessary for the inspection. He was hoping to elicit another squeal from the girl so that he could have the grand pleasure of spanking her again. But alas, the little initiate stayed silent throughout the rest of the ordeal.

After the High Priest gave Peggy one last slap on her plump buttocks, he commenced to inspect the other girls in the same manner, the only difference being that neither uttered a sound. He gave them each one or two hardy slaps on their backsides, and a tingling pat on their pussies.

When the High Priest announced that he was done with the girls, now standing naked, he ordered a slave, Gilean, to take them and bathe them.

Gilean silently rose from the cushions in the corner and came toward them, beckoning them to follow. The girls did so without hesitation.

Although the experience had frightened them, all three girls had a glow of excitation on their faces, their eyes shining as they followed Gilean down yet another torchlit narrow hallway.

They entered into a long room with a large steaming pool in its center. Gilean led the way, and soon the girls were immersed in the warm water. Bernadette couldn't contain herself any longer, and drifting toward Brigeen she whispered, "I am so excited I could nearly die!"

Suddenly Gilean leapt out of the water and went to a wall where a row of long leather whips hung in a neat row. She pointed them out, and that was all. None of the girls spoke another word as they bathed.

After washing, they were led to a small antechamber warmed by rocks and fire. Gilean tossed some water from a bowl next to the rocks and the room

146

became warmer and steam-filled. She stretched her perfect legs out along a narrow rock shelf and lay down. The girls silently followed suit.

The four of them lay there for some time, until the wait was almost unbearable. Brigeen was certain that she would faint; everything around her became like a strange hallucination. She looked over at her young companions and could tell by their glazed eyes that they were feeling the same.

When she thought she would scream from the heat and claustrophobia of the low room, Brigeen was helped up by the strong hand of Gilean. They exchanged glances, and there was a reassuring glow in Gilean's black eyes that made Brigeen feel calm.

Gilean then led the three of them to yet another chamber in the amazing underground network where the girls were handed beautiful gauze robes. Gilean patiently helped each girl into the flowing dress, and then she softly brushed and braided their hair, weaving sacred oak leaves into wreaths that were placed on their heads. When she was done, Gilean stood back and admired her work. Oddly, she remained naked the entire time.

The three young girls looked beautiful. They turned to one another to stare happily into each other's eyes, marvelling at each other's glowing skin. The soft flesh of their bodies could be seen delicately through the transparent fabric. They were ready for the Festival at last.

# -12-

The High Priestess was raging on this night, the Festival of Venus. She was hungry for some virgin pussy. It seemed that each year lasted longer and longer, and the Festival came more slowly each time. The fever welled inside her chest and the desire made her cruel.

But soon, she thought, a matter of hours, I will have more flesh writhing in front of me than I know what to do with. I will have new consorts by morning. This thought quelled the rage that was building inside her.

She lay back against the down pillows on her bed. Her fourposter bed was made completely from stone. Each carved post featured the Sheila-Na-Gig, the great Creatress, and Destroyer. The Sheila was the High Priestess' chosen symbol. It always showed an old crone with a terrifying scowl on her aged face. She always was depicted crouching, exposing her enormous genitalia.

The High Priestess stared at the strange figures on

149

the ominous posts of her bed. They used to be all over Ireland, she thought sadly, regarding her favorite symbol of the Old Way. The idiotic Church destroyed her. She laughed aloud at the thought. The Church could not destroy the High Priestess.

She dozed, and when she woke she rang a large brass gong beside her bed. It was time that she was prepared for the Festival. Four young novices—two women, two men—arrived, their heads obediently bowed.

"I must prepare," she said bluntly, and the novices quickly set to work arranging the magical pungent oils and the ritual dress of the defloration ceremony.

The Priestess put on a sheath of gold chain metal. It fit her so tightly the beautiful curve of her ass was completely accentuated. It made a slight clinking sound as she walked. She would leave her perfect breasts bare, as was the ancient tradition. The novices wove her hair with saffron buds, the herb of the Great Goddess; her hair was perfumed with a heavy musk. Her fingernails were filed to points. Her torso was oiled by the hands of the young male novices.

When she stood back and looked at her reflection in the giant mirror in her chamber, she smiled wickedly, knowing that she was the most beautiful and powerful woman in all Europe.

The reflection showed a tall woman, in her mid-twenties. Her red hair fell in cascading locks to her knees. Her oiled breasts stood firm and high, the tiny aureoles nearly brown, the small nipples erect from the warmth of the fragrant oil. Her eyes, piercing green almonds, were made more fierce by the sinister slant of her elegant eyebrows. The gilded sheath she wore exposed her flat brown belly, the waist of the skirt sitting right above the line where the curls of

150

her pubic hair began. She smiled at her own magnificent reflection. Her full lips turned up at the corners, the smile revealing the sharp structure of her cheeks, the dramatic lighting making the jut of the fine bones more exaggerated. She rubbed a long finger languorously over one nipple and then the other, then over the smooth flesh of her belly.

Yes, I am beautiful she thought without shame. Only those worth her time were initiated into the Arts of Love and the Secrets of the Old Way. She hoped she would not be disappointed with the newly arrived initiates. She so needed new consorts.

At last the High Priest, her brother, entered the chamber to escort her to the great hall where the festival had already started, the worshippers already in frenetic activity. The two exited together, arm in arm.

# -13-

The fire cast weird shadows over the undulating bodies in the cave. Moans and screams echoed in the strange cavern. Music could be heard over the cries.

The regal Priestess stood with her attendants on the huge stone dais overlooking the night's events. She was shining with an eerie glow. The orange light showed the walls of the huge cavern lined with the naked bodies of young women. They were held against the stone walls with iron bolts threaded with leather manacles. Devotees, both men and women, worshipped the bodies that hung there.

She observed as leather thongs came hissing down on the oiled flesh of many of the girls. They were writhing beautifully. She saw that clamps had been attached to the nipples of others and were pulling the soft flesh. Some of the women pinned to the wall were enjoying the tongues of their tormentors, while others had the pleasure of a cock or a fist. At the foot of this spectacle, worshippers could be seen writhing on the ground. Over one hundred bodies mingled. Beautiful women sucked voraciously the cocks of men whose hips thrust up and down. Hands on quivering wet pussy lips made women scream, racked with delight. Women melted together sucking one another, breasts gleaming, teeth flashing. Every possible combination and position was effected. The initiated were making a fine showing tonight.

They all moved to the frenzied pace of the queer music that filled the space. Cries of pleasure and pain rang out. The center of the cave looked like one enormous writhing snake, as devotees pleased and serviced one another on this festival night. The light of the fires reflected on the high vaulted ceiling of the cavern.

The wine was working to bring the people to a state of possession, as the members of the ancient cult brought one another to states of ecstasy over and over in an attempt to maintain a perpetual state of orgasmic pleasure. This was ordered by their religion.

The High Priestess was pleased with the triumph of the night. She was flanked on either side by four young men who stood naked and chained. She held their leashes in her hand. She was surveying the collective body of her people in order to pick the most fetching young female to service her during the defloration ceremony. Her eyes wandered over so much naked and undulating flesh. It would be hard to choose. There were some beautiful, tantalizing creatures, both shackled to the cave wall, and amongst those worshipping on the stone floor of the temple. She would have to choose one soon. The virgins were waiting in the antechamber, being served the potent red wine and attended to by Phelim. Ah, Phelim, thought the Priestess, sighing, I would love to get him to stay on the Isle. He is such a wonderful cock some nights...and such a powerful magician.

The commanding woman cast her eyes about the hall. She saw a young girl of perhaps seventeen. She was a tall lean woman, with deep brown skin. Her chestnut hair hung in long tresses about her perfect breast. She was astride a young man riding his cock furiously, her hips moving powerfully over his. Another young woman with blond tresses was sucking the clit of the dark girl. She sprawled over the man's muscular chest as she was in turn tickled by his tongue. Two younger women, not as pretty as the dark girl, toyed with the dark girl's high breasts. She was bucking like a wild animal in order to impale herself more violently on the man's prick. It seemed that all the energy of this coupling emanated from her powerful body. She arched her back, and dragging her fingernails into the other girl's back, she screamed out loud in total abandon, nearly drawing blood from the flesh of the girl beneath her.

The dark girl took no pause and lifted herself off the red and still-engorged member of the heaving man. His cock gleamed with cum, and she flung herself upon it, licking any leftover cream. She then fell atop the fair girl and began to slap her breasts violently with one hand, the other opening the lips of her dark red flower. The fair girl squirmed under the weight of the body atop her, and the dark girl fell to ravishing the blond girl's breasts. Another well-muscled young man had come upon them and had pushed open the dark girl's buttocks. He ran his tongue lightly over the small rosy aperture, and the dark girl moaned in delighted response. She began to nip and suck the blonde girl's breasts harder. The man raised his hips to her ass and pulled the beautiful firm flesh to his pulsing cock. This wondrous dark girl fell back onto his member with glee and began to rotate her hips, allowing him to penetrate her fully in that more narrow passage. All the while she maintained her torment of the girl beneath her, kissing and biting her. Finally, wriggling down her stomach, the dark-haired beauty plunged her tongue deep inside the blonde bush of the younger girl.

"She's magnificent," said the High Priestess to her brother. "I want her to service me as the defloration ceremony goes on. I do so need a wanton young wench to lap adoringly at my cunt while I watch the young ones scream with delight as they are penetrated for the first time. Shall I pick someone for you, brother?"

The High Priest declined, preferring his usual slave to suck his cock during the delights of the ritual to come.

The High Priestess turned to one of the attendants on the end of the chain. "Fetch her," she said coldly, pointing to the dark girl who was now hungrily taking the full length of a man's cock down her throat, while another man ate her pussy. With her free hand the dark girl lightly slapped the open sex of a woman new to the grouping.

"Bring her here now," she said releasing the young man's chains.

The music continued. The whips fell on yielding flesh, and constant screams of orgiastic pleasure continued to rise and fall with the beating drums.

The dark girl was brought before the High Priestess. She knelt with respect. The Priestess grabbed her roughly by the shoulder and pulled the girl abruptly toward her. It was obvious the dark girl was frightened. This only heightened the Queen's passion. She pinched the girl's already hardened nipples. She thrust her hand between the girl's strong brown thighs. They were dripping from all the pleasure on the cavern floor.

"Down!" ordered the High Priestess, and the girl immediately dropped to her knees. The Priestess sat back in her chair and, unclasping her sheath, she reached out and shoved the beautiful girl's face in between her own wet thighs. The girl started sucking hungrily. The Priestess sighed. Turning to her brother she said, "Let me taste the virgins before they are deflowered. I do so love the taste of virgin juices."

The High Priest turned and rang an enormous gong, and from a door in the stone wall the new initiates came forth. They were all clad in the ritual white robes, their hair decorated, their bodies scented. They walked in a line connected by a silver chain that ran together, connected at the collars they all wore.

Bernadette, Brigeen and Peggy all flushed at the sight they beheld. The bodies continued to writhe on the ground before them. The three girls looked in wonder at the women strapped to the chamber walls. Then they raised their bewildered eyes to the balcony.

Bernadette could not hold back an audible sigh at the sight of the magnificent High Priestess. There she sat, her thighs spread far apart, the strong back of a dark girl between her thighs, the girl's face buried in the depths of the Priestess' spread legs.

"Bring them to me," the Priestess called. The gong was sounded again, and as the young initiates filed by, the wild activity on the floor slowed to a stop. By the time the virgins had reached the balcony to stand with the Priestess the eyes of all the worshippers were on them.

The three girls looked at one another affectionately. The Priestess said almost gently, "Phelim, my love, bring one of those young beauties forth so that I can

157

place my lips on her virgin sex. It will be the last kiss before she is no longer unconsecrated."

Phelim silently tugged at Brigeen's silver collar. She approached the chair of the Priestess. The dark girl continued to suck and lick her pussy, yet the Priestess hardly seemed to notice. She told Brigeen to stand on either wide arm of her stone chair. Brigeen complied immediately. When she'd climbed up, her copse of dark curls was at the level of the Priestess' mouth.

When Brigeen felt the magical tongue of the Great Goddess on her virgin nether lips, she thought she might explode with joy. Never, never, had Brigeen felt such a powerful sensation. The long tongue of the Priestess explored the depth of her cleft; she could hear herself moaning with pleasure as she thrust against the mouth of the Queen. Time seemed to stop. Her pleasure was complete in moments, her body trembling with powerful orgasmic tremors.

She was helped down from her perch by two attendants. She felt delirious. She was on fire. Brigeen hardly heard the Queen say, "Now, my delicious little one, approach the man of your choice and grant him the token of your lips. He will be the one to take you."

As if in a dream, she drifted to the magnificent Phelim, and placed a wet kiss on his lips. She could hear the Priestess laugh and commend her on her choice.

Brigeen stood back, dazed, and watched the High Priestess bestow her magic kiss on all the new initiates. She saw that each had the same experience as she. She watched Bernadette's small hips move furiously for only the briefest moment as she straddled the High Priestess' chair. Bernadette selected Joe, the splendid young man they had serviced in Dublin so long ago. Peggy selected one of the beautiful Scandinavian boys to have her virginity.

After each of the initiates had been given the secret kiss of the Priestess, they were ready to engage in their first sexual union.

The drums began to beat slowly. Phelim approached Brigeen and quickly tore her robe from her. He whispered to her, "How I've wanted you since we first met. I wanted to fuck you so that you screamed. Now's my chance, love. I am going to make you cry out in desperation; I'm going to take you so hard. You will never forget it." And with that he began to suckle her lovely round breasts as he tore at his own robes, until they were both naked. Brigeen chanced to look over to see Bernadette and Joe also naked kissing furiously, Bernadette's little hand running hungrily over his stiff cock. He was opening her pussy lips and displaying the wet lining of her flesh.

The sight so aroused Brigeen that she turned to Phelim, and whispered heavily, "Oh...do...do it now! I want to feel you in me. Please."

But Phelim continued to tease her breasts, her pubic hair, and flicked her throbbing little clit until she was dripping and writhing against the wonderful hardness of his body. She could feel his stiff member against her thigh. He lifted her. With one arm around her he held her over his raging penis, teasing her pulsing cunt with the tip of his cock. Brigeen was wriggling her legs around the small of Phelim's back, wanting to thrust her body down on his large sex, to feel him fill her up, give her pain. She wanted him to take her wretched virginity.

Suddenly, Phelim released his grip, and she went crashing down on top of his cock. It slid into her slippery pussy with one violent thrust. She threw her head back and screamed. She was certain that she was going to be split in two. She cried out again and again as Phelim lifted her body up and down wildly on his thrusting hips. Her breasts brushed against his chest. She felt so many sensations that soon her screams turned to moans of pleasure as she was brought up and down again on Phelim's impressive shaft.

Meanwhile, her closest companion was straddling Joe. Bernadette rode him with such expertise and energy, her boyish hips rocking with delight, her cries loud and full, that one would have suspected her virginity if it weren't for the virgin blood that one could see as she rose and fell wildly over her partner.

The Scandinavian had approached Peggy from behind and entered her cunt this way. He pushed deeper and deeper into the screaming girl, all the while teasing her clit with one hand, her tits with another.

The other virgins struck various poses of coupling, presenting a lovely picture for the Priestess who now was writhing under the tireless tongue of the dark girl.

Brigeen could feel herself about to come. She pressed the muscles in her thighs together as Phelim's wonderful huge cock slid in and out of her furiously. His fingers were tickling the rosette of her asshole as her cheeks spread, her legs wrapped around him. "I'm coming my love! Ah...I'm coming!" She heard herself scream. She felt so much pleasure, she was not sure if it were real. And then she felt the heat of her orgasm. She felt Phelim thrust so deep she felt that he was touching her spine with the tip of his penis. He was making hoarse moans, and she felt his body tense with hers. A moment longer and they were lost together in a dark abyss of total pleasure.

The High Priestess was jerking in wild pleasure under the tongue of the dark girl, stimulated by the sight of the beautiful young virgins squirming and screaming under the powerful thrusts of their partners. When the Priestess climaxed, all the other couples began shrieking and wildly bucking with wild pleasure.

The drums beat their steady rhythm, and because the High Priestess had climaxed, the worshippers fell to their orgy once again with renewed relish because of the beauty of the defloration of the young ones on the high balcony.

# *EPILOGUE*

The day after the dreamlike sensuality of the defloration, the three girls woke in a dark stone chamber. They were lying together on a large bed covered with fur. They all felt disoriented. The entire night before had been filled with uncontrolled fucking. Each girl had taken several partners during the worship, each being held in a total state of pleasure until she had dropped from exhaustion and excitement.

Quite suddenly, the High Priestess entered the room. She was dressed in a plain white robe. She addressed the three girls who sprawled naked on the bed. She told them that they would be invited to stay on as her personal consorts, so great had been the pleasure they afforded her the night before.

There was one condition; they would have to agree to be branded, as were all the consorts of the High Priestess.

It was the mark that they had seen on Mary at the Lord Master's home. The girls agreed to the privilege.

That same evening, in the dead of night, they were taken to a most secret chamber and marked for life as the consorts and lovers of the High Priestess, an unsurpassed honor in the rites of the Old Ways.

It was a nightmarish scene as Bernadette, Brigeen, and Peggy were strapped to the wall with leather thongs. The fire glowed, heating the small branding iron bearing the seal of the High Priestess. The screams of pain and fear were genuine as the iron touched the soft flesh of the young girls. The echoes of their shrieks rang throughout the underground

162

caves. The High Priestess sat in a chair observing the ritual, smiling evilly, and slowly, sensuously masturbating as each girl underwent her torments.

Bernadette, Peggy, and Brigeen were never seen again in Dublin, having finally left behind the world of the uninitiated.

# HELP US TO PLAN THE FUTURE
# OF EROTIC FICTION –

### – and no stamp required!

**The Nexus Library** is Britain's largest and fastest-growing collection of erotic fiction. We'd like your help to make it even bigger and better.

Like many of our books, the questionnaire below is completely anonymous, so don't feel shy about telling us what you really think. We want to know what kind of people our readers are – we want to know what you like about Nexus books, what you dislike, and what changes you'd like to see.

Just answer the questions on the following pages in the spaces provided; if more than one person would like to take part, please feel free to photocopy the questionnaire. Then tear the pages from the book and send them in an envelope to the address at the end of the questionnaire. No stamp is required.

---

## THE NEXUS QUESTIONNAIRE

SECTION ONE: ABOUT YOU ✍

.1 Sex *(yes, of course, but try to be serious for just a moment)*
  Male ☐  Female ☐

2 Age
  under 21 ☐  21 – 30 ☐
  31 – 40 ☐  41 – 50 ☐
  51 – 60 ☐  over 60 ☐

3 At what age did you leave full-time education?
  still in education ☐  16 or younger ☐
  17 – 19 ☐  20 or older ☐

4 Occupation _____

5 Annual household income
  under £10,000 ☐  £10–£20,000 ☐
  £20–£30,000 ☐  £30–£40,000 ☐
  over £40,000 ☐

1.6 Where do you live?
*Please write in the county in which you live (for example Hampshire), or the city if you live in a large metropolitan area (for example Manchester)* _____

---

## SECTION TWO : ABOUT BUYING NEXUS BOOKS

2.1 How did you acquire this book?
I bought it myself ☐  My partner bought it ☐
I borrowed it / found it ☐

2.2 If this book was bought ...
... in which town or city? _____
... in what sort of shop:  High Street bookshop ☐
local newsagent ☐
at a railway station ☐
at an airport ☐
at motorway services ☐
other: _____

2.3 Have you ever had difficulty finding Nexus books on sale?
Yes ☐  No ☐
If you have had difficulty in buying Nexus books, where would you like to be able to buy them?
... in which town or city _____
... in what sort of shop from list in previous question _____

2.4 Have you ever been reluctant to buy a Nexus book because of the sexual nature of the cover picture?
Yes ☐  No ☐

2.5 Please tick which of the following statements you agree with
I find some Nexus cover pictures offensive / too blatant ☐

I would be less embarassed about buying Nexus books if the cover pictures were less blatant ☐

I think that in general the pictures on Nexus books are about right ☐

I think Nexus cover pictures should be as sexy as possible ☐

## SECTION THREE: ABOUT NEXUS BOOKS

3.1 How many Nexus books do you own? _____

3.2 Roughly how many Nexus books have you read? _____

3.3 What are your three favourite Nexus books?
First choice _____
Second Choice _____
Third Choice _____

3.4 What are your three favourite Nexus cover pictures?
First choice _____
Second choice _____
Third choice _____

## SECTION FOUR: ABOUT YOUR IDEAL EROTIC NOVEL

We want to publish books you want to read – so this is your chance to tell us exactly what your ideal erotic novel would be like.

4.1 Using a scale of 1 to 5 (1 = no interest at all, 5 = your ideal), please rate the following possible settings for an erotic novel:
Medieval/barbarian/sword 'n' sorcery ☐
Renaissance/Elizabethan/Restoration ☐
Victorian/Edwardian ☐
1920s & 1930s – the Jazz Age ☐
Present day ☐
Future/Science Fiction ☐

4.2 Using the same scale of 1 to 5, please rate the following styles in which an erotic novel could be written:
Realistic, down to earth, set in real life ☐
Escapist fantasy, but just about believable ☐
Completely unreal, impressionistic, dreamlike ☐

4.3 Would you prefer your ideal erotic novel to be written from the viewpoint of the main male characters or the main female characters?
Male ☐    Female ☐

4.4 Is there one particular setting or subject matter that your ideal erotic novel would contain?
_____

## SECTION FIVE: LAST WORDS

5.1    What do you like best about Nexus books?

_____

_____

5.2    What do you most dislike about Nexus books?

_____

_____

5.3    In what way, if any, would you like to change Nexus covers?

_____

_____

5.4    Here's a space for any other comments:

_____

_____

_____

_____

_____

_____

_____

---

*Thank you for completing this questionnaire. Now tear it out of the book – carefully! – put it in an envelope and send it to:*

**Nexus Books**
**FREEPOST**
**London**
**W10 5BR**

*No stamp is required.*

# THE BEST IN EROTIC READING – BY POST

The Nexus Library of Erotica – over a hundred volumes – is available from many booksellers and newsagents. If you have any difficulty obtaining the books you require, you can order them by post. Photocopy the list below, or tear the list out of the book; then tick the titles you want and fill in the form at the end of the list. Titles marked 1992 are not yet available: please do not try to order them – just look out for them in the shops!

## EDWARDIAN, VICTORIAN & OLDER EROTICA

| | | | |
|---|---|---|---|
| ADVENTURES OF A SCHOOLBOY | Anonymous | £3.99 | |
| THE AUTOBIOGRAPHY OF A FLEA | Anonymous | £2.99 | |
| BEATRICE | Anonymous | £3.99 | |
| THE BOUDOIR | Anonymous | £3.99 | |
| THE DIARY OF A CHAMBERMAID | Mirabeau | £2.99 | |
| THE LIFTED CURTAIN | Mirabeau | £3.50 | |
| EVELINE | Anonymous | £2.99 | |
| MORE EVELINE | Anonymous | £3.99 | |
| FESTIVAL OF VENUS | Anonymous | £4.50 | 1992 |
| FRANK' & I | Anonymous | £2.99 | |
| GARDENS OF DESIRE | Roger Rougiere | £4.50 | 1992 |
| OH, WICKED COUNTRY | Anonymous | £3.50 | |
| LASCIVIOUS SCENES | Anonymous | £4.50 | 1992 |
| THE LASCIVIOUS MONK | Anonymous | £2.99 | |
| LAURA MIDDLETON | Anonymous | £3.99 | |
| A MAN WITH A MAID 1 | Anonymous | £3.50 | |
| A MAN WITH A MAID 2 | Anonymous | £3.50 | |
| A MAN WITH A MAID 3 | Anonymous | £3.50 | |
| MAUDIE | Anonymous | £2.99 | |
| THE MEMOIRS OF DOLLY MORTON | Anonymous | £3.99 | |

| | | | |
|---|---|---|---|
| A NIGHT IN A MOORISH HAREM | Anonymous | £3.99 | |
| PARISIAN FROLICS | Anonymous | £2.99 | |
| PLEASURE BOUND | Anonymous | £3.99 | |
| THE PLEASURES OF LOLOTTE | Andrea de Nerciat | £3.99 | |
| THE PRIMA DONNA | Anonymous | £2.99 | |
| RANDIANA | Anonymous | £4.50 | |
| REGINE | E.K. | £2.99 | |
| THE ROMANCE OF LUST 1 | Anonymous | £3.99 | |
| THE ROMANCE OF LUST 2 | Anonymous | £2.99 | |
| ROSA FIELDING | Anonymous | £2.99 | |
| SUBURBAN SOULS 1 | Anonymous | £2.99 | |
| SUBURBAN SOULS 2 | Anonymous | £2.50 | |
| THREE TIMES A WOMAN | Anonymous | £2.99 | |
| THE TWO SISTERS | Anonymous | £3.99 | |
| VIOLETTE | Anonymous | £2.99 | |

## "THE JAZZ AGE"

| | | | |
|---|---|---|---|
| ALTAR OF VENUS | Anonymous | £2.99 | |
| THE SECRET GARDEN ROOM | Georgette de la Tour | £3.50 | |
| BEHIND THE BEADED CURTAIN | Georgette de la Tour | £3.50 | |
| BLANCHE | Anonymous | £3.99 | |
| BLUE ANGEL NIGHTS | Margarete von Falkensee | £2.99 | |
| BLUE ANGEL DAYS | Margarete von Falkensee | £3.99 | |
| BLUE ANGEL SECRETS | Margarete von Falkensee | £2.99 | |
| CAROUSEL | Anonymous | £3.99 | |
| CONFESSIONS OF AN ENGLISH MAID | Anonymous | £3.99 | |
| FLOSSIE | Anonymous | £2.50 | |
| SABINE | Anonymous | £3.99 | |
| PLAISIR D'AMOUR | Anne-Marie Villefranche | £2.99 | |
| FOLIES D'AMOUR | Anne-Marie Villefranche | £2.99 | |
| JOIE D'AMOUR | Anne-Marie Villefranche | £3.99 | |
| MYSTERE D'AMOUR | Anne-Marie Villefranche | £3.99 | |
| SECRETS D'AMOUR | Anne-Marie Villefranche | £3.50 | |
| SOUVENIR D'AMOUR | Anne-Marie Villefranche | £3.99 | |
| SPIES IN SILK | Piers Falconer | £4.50 | 1992 |

## CONTEMPORARY EROTICA

| | | | |
|---|---|---|---|
| AMAZONS | Erin Caine | £3.99 | 1992 |
| COCKTAILS | Stanley Carten | £3.99 | |
| CITY OF ONE-NIGHT STANDS | Stanley Carten | £4.50 | 1992 |
| CONTOURS OF DARKNESS | Marco Vassi | £3.50 | |
| THE GENTLE DEGENERATES | Marco Vassi | £3.99 | |

| | | | |
|---|---|---|---|
| MIND BLOWER | Marco Vassi | £3.50 | |
| THE SALINE SOLUTION | Marco Vassi | £2.99 | |
| DARK FANTASIES | Nigel Anthony | £3.99 | |
| THE DAYS AND NIGHTS OF MIGUMI | P.M. | £3.99 | |
| THE LATIN LOVER | P.M. | £3.99 | |
| THE DEVIL'S ADVOCATE | Anonymous | £3.99 | |
| DIPLOMATIC SECRETS | Antoine Lelouche | £3.50 | |
| DIPLOMATIC PLEASURES | Antoine Lelouche | £3.50 | |
| DIPLOMATIC DIVERSIONS | Antoine Lelouche | £3.99 | 1992 |
| ENGINE OF DESIRE | Alexis Arven | £3.99 | |
| DIRTY WORK | Alexis Arven | £3.99 | |
| DREAMS OF FAIR WOMEN | Celeste Arden | £2.99 | |
| THE FANTASY HUNTERS | Celeste Arden | £3.99 | |
| A GALLERY OF NUDES | Anthony Grey | £4.50 | |
| THE GIRL FROM PAGE 3 | Mike Angelo | £3.99 | |
| THE INSTITUTE | Maria del Rey | £3.99 | 1992 |
| LAURE-ANNE | Laure-Anne | £2.99 | |
| LAURE-ANNE ENCORE | Laure-Anne | £2.99 | |
| LAURE-ANNE TOUJOURS | Laure-Anne | £3.50 | |
| Ms DEEDES AT HOME | Carole Andrews | £4.50 | 1992 |
| MY SEX MY SOUL | Amelia Greene | £2.99 | |
| ONE WEEK IN THE PRIVATE HOUSE | Esme Ombreux | £3.99 | |
| PALACE OF SWEETHEARTS | Delver Maddingley | £4.50 | 1992 |
| THE SECRET WEB | Jane-Anne Roberts | £3.50 | |
| STEPHANIE | Susanna Hughes | £3.99 | |
| STEPHANIE'S CASTLE | Susanna Hughes | £4.50 | 1992 |
| THE DOMINO TATTOO | Cyrian Amberlake | £3.99 | |
| THE DOMINA ENIGMA | Cyrian Amberlake | £3.99 | |
| THE DOMINO QUEEN | Cyrian Amberlake | £3.99 | |

## EROTIC SCIENCE FICTION

| | | | |
|---|---|---|---|
| PLEASUREHOUSE 13 | Agnetha Anders | £3.99 | |
| THE LAST DAYS OF THE PLEASUREHOUSE | Agnetha Anders | £4.50 | 1992 |
| WICKED | Andrea Arven | £3.99 | |
| WILD | Andrea Arven | £4.50 | 1992 |

## ANCIENT & FANTASY SETTINGS

| | | | |
|---|---|---|---|
| CHAMPIONS OF LOVE | Anonymous | £3.99 | |
| CHAMPIONS OF DESIRE | Anonymous | £3.50 | |
| CHAMPIONS OF PLEASURE | Anonymous | £3.50 | |
| THE SLAVE OF LIDIR | Aran Ashe | £3.99 | |
| THE DUNGEONS OF LIDIR | Aran Ashe | £3.99 | |

| | | | |
|---|---|---|---|
| THE FOREST OF BONDAGE | Aran Ashe | £3.99 | |
| PLEASURE ISLAND | Aran Ashe | £4.50 | 1992 |
| ROMAN ORGY | Marcus van Heller | £4.50 | 1992 |

## CONTEMPORARY FRENCH EROTICA (translated into English)

| | | | |
|---|---|---|---|
| EXPLOITS OF A YOUNG DON JUAN | Anonymous | £2.99 | |
| INDISCREET MEMOIRS | Alain Dorval | £2.99 | |
| INSTRUMENT OF PLEASURE | Celeste Piano | £3.99 | |
| JOY | Joy Laurey | £2.99 | |
| JOY AND JOAN | Joy Laurey | £2.99 | |
| JOY IN LOVE | Joy Laurey | £2.75 | |
| LILIANE | Paul Verguin | £3.50 | |
| MANDOLINE | Anonymous | £3.99 | |
| LUST IN PARIS | Antoine S. | £2.99 | |
| NYMPH IN PARIS | Galia S. | £2.99 | |
| SCARLET NIGHTS | Juan Muntaner | £3.99 | |
| SENSUAL LIAISONS | Anonymous | £3.50 | |
| SENSUAL SECRETS | Anonymous | £3.99 | |
| THE NEW STORY OF O | Anonymous | £3.50 | |
| THE IMAGE | Jean de Berg | £3.99 | 1992 |
| VIRGINIE | Nathalie Perreau | £4.50 | 1992 |
| THE PAPER WOMAN | Francoise Rey | £4.50 | 1992 |

## SAMPLERS & COLLECTIONS

| | | | |
|---|---|---|---|
| EROTICON | ed. J-P Spencer | £3.99 | |
| EROTICON 2 | ed. J-P Spencer | £3.99 | |
| EROTICON 3 | ed. J-P Spencer | £2.99 | |
| EROTICON 4 | ed. J-P Spencer | £3.99 | |
| THE FIESTA LETTERS | ed. Chris Lloyd | £2.99 | |
| THE PLEASURES OF LOVING | ed. Maren Sell | £2.99 | |

## NON-FICTION

| | | | |
|---|---|---|---|
| HOW TO DRIVE YOUR MAN WILD IN BED | Graham Masterton | £3.99 | |
| HOW TO DRIVE YOUR WOMAN WILD IN BED | Graham Masterton | £3.99 | |
| HOW TO BE THE PERFECT LOVER | Graham Masterton | £2.99 | |
| FEMALE SEXUAL AWARENESS | Barry & Emily McCarthy | £4.99 | |
| WHAT MEN WANT | Susan Crain Bakos | £3.99 | |
| YOUR SEXUAL SECRETS | Marty Klein | £3.99 | |

------------------------------------------------------------

Please send me the books I have ticked above.

Name    .................................................

Address   .................................................

             .................................................

       .......................Post code  .............

Send to: **Nexus Books Cash Sales, PO Box 11, Falmouth, Cornwall, TR10 9EN**

Please enclose a cheque or postal order, made payable to **Nexus Books**, to the value of the books you have ordered plus postage and packing costs as follows:

    UK and BFPO – £1.00 for the first book, 50p for the second book, and 30p for each subsequent book to a maximum of £3.00;

    Overseas (including Republic of Ireland) – £2.00 for the first book, £1.00 for the second book, and 50p for each subsequent book.

If you would prefer to pay by VISA or ACCESS/MASTERCARD, please write your card number here:

_ _ _ _    _ _ _ _    _ _ _ _    _ _ _ _

Signature:   _____